ARMY BRATS

ARMY BRATS

DAPHNE BENEDIS-GRAB

Scholastic Press / New York

Library of Congress Cataloging-in-Publication Data

Names: Benedis-Grab, Daphne, author.
Title: Army brats / Daphne Benedis-Grab.
Description: First edition. | New York, NY : Scholastic Press, 2017. |
Summary: When the Bailey family moves into an army base in Virginia, there are a lot of adjustments to make; twelve-year-old Tom runs afoul of the base school bully, ten-year-old Charlotte finds herself trying too hard to make friends with the "cool" girls, and six-year-old Rosie is just being difficult as usual--but they come together to investigate a mysterious building full of weird cages, and uncover Fort Patrick's secrets.
Identifiers: LCCN 2016031951 (print) | LCCN 2016039648 (ebook) |
ISBN 9780545932059 (hardcover) | ISBN 9780545932073
Subjects: LCSH: Families of military personnel—Virginia—Juvenile fiction. | Brothers and sisters—Juvenile fiction. | Middle schools—Juvenile fiction. | Military bases, American—Virginia—Juvenile fiction. | Bullying—Juvenile fiction. | Secrecy—Juvenile fiction. | Virginia—Juvenile fiction. | CYAC: Children of military personnel—Fiction. | Brothers and sisters—Fiction. | Middle schools—Fiction. | Schools—Fiction. | Military bases—Fiction. | Bullying—Fiction. | Secrets—Fiction. | Virginia—Fiction.
Classification: LCC PZ7.B43233 Ar 2017 (print) |
LCC PZ7.B43233 (ebook) | DDC 813.6 [Fic]—dc23
LC record available at https://lccn.loc.gov/2016031951

10 9 8 7 6 5 4 3 2 1   17 18 19 20 21

Printed in the U.S.A.   23
First edition, April 2017

Book design by Mary Claire Cruz

For Erlan

The light-blue minivan carrying the Bailey family, their dog, Cupcake, and their most essential belongings, was cruising up the winding mountain road shaded by pine, aspen, and black walnut trees, when a loud shout burst from the way back.

"Stop the car!" Rosie, the youngest Bailey, hollered. "We have a DEFCON twenty-seven back here."

"There's no such thing as DEFCON twenty-seven," twelve-year-old Tom announced wearily to Rosie while Dad pulled the van to the side of the road. Rosie had recently decided to start using army lingo in honor of the family's move to Fort Patrick. The problem was that Rosie kept forgetting the right terms and making up her own, confusing everyone.

"And I don't think Cupcake needing a pit stop is a DEFCON anything," Charlotte added as she fumbled with the car door. She'd been getting carsick from the twisty road, so she was first to scramble out of the van.

"Smell that mountain air," Dad said appreciatively as the rest of the family piled out onto the side of the road.

All Charlotte smelled was a bunch of trees, but she nodded anyway.

"Good for the lungs," he went on, pounding his chest for a moment and then coughing a bit.

Charlotte looked at Tom and they both giggled.

"Don't know my own strength, do I?" Dad asked cheerfully, his dark red hair blowing slightly in the breeze. Thanks to Dad, Tom and Charlotte were redheads too, but while Dad and Tom had hair that was like burnished copper, Charlotte's was a light strawberry blond that came with pale skin and freckles she hated almost as much as the sunscreen she had to slather on every time she stepped out into sunlight.

"Did anyone see my sunglasses?" Dad asked. "I think they slid into the backseat when we took that sharp turn outside of DC."

Charlotte looked in the van. The big plastic glasses Dad claimed were stylish—despite Rosie's insistence on calling them clown glasses—were resting just under her seat. She reached in and grabbed them.

"Thanks, sweetie," Dad said, taking them from

her. "And I like your nails—very appropriate for the occasion."

Charlotte grinned as she held out a hand so Dad could fully admire the tiny white army stars she'd painted on each nail in honor of their move. She loved giving herself fancy and unusual manicures and had a big collection of brightly colored polish.

"Very snazzy," Dad said, which made both Tom and Charlotte snort a bit. Dad was big on old-fashioned words like *snazzy*.

"How much longer till we get there?" Charlotte asked. She wasn't sure if it was the mountain air or just standing on solid ground, but the swirling in her stomach was settling down.

"About fifteen more minutes," Tom answered. Charlotte knew he had been keeping a close eye on the GPS guiding them toward their new home—she was familiar with all of Tom's travel habits since their family, like all army families, relocated so often.

Charlotte, who had recently turned ten and three quarters and now officially considered herself eleven, was always dismayed when her parents announced a move. No matter how often it happened, it was hard to leave friends and the familiar behind for a new, uncertain future. The one thing that made the moves easier, of course, was her siblings. They might fight sometimes, but walking into school on the first day was always a million times easier with Tom by her side. Though even that thought made Charlotte anxious, because this year Tom, who had dyslexia, was getting extra help at lunch, leaving Charlotte to face the cafeteria on her own for the first time ever. And she was dreading that.

"I think we're all set," Mom said, leading the way out of the woods. She was dressed in khaki pants and a soft T-shirt, but Charlotte knew that as soon as they reached the base, Mom would change into her officer's uniform to report for duty.

"Roger that," Dad said, giving Rosie a high five. Delicate Rosie, with her heart-shaped face and silky black hair, looked like a tiny angel. But in her case, looks were quite deceiving.

Charlotte remembered when Mom had sent home the photo of three-year-old Rosie, whom she had met on the streets of Beijing, China. Rosie had slipped away from the orphanage where she lived so she could spend the afternoon pretending to be a dog, darting about and nipping people on the ankle. Everyone else on the sidewalk was annoyed, but Mom fell instantly in love and decided their family was the perfect fit for the energetic toddler barking up a storm. Since Rosie was an older child (and, Charlotte had always suspected, because Rosie was so high energy), the adoption was expedited. Before they knew it, the Baileys had become a family of five.

If Rosie had turned out to be as sugar sweet as that first photo promised, things might not have worked out so well. But Rosie had the mind and wits of a super-villain, and much to the admiration of her new siblings, quickly established herself as a force to be reckoned with.

And now, as Charlotte climbed back into the van, she knew she couldn't imagine life without Rosie. Even if she was driving everyone crazy with her new army terms.

Rosie settled into the backseat, Cupcake's head in her lap. "Mom does everyone on post get to fly around in birdies?" Rosie asked. Ever since she had found out about the move, Rosie was full of questions about life on base.

"Helicopters are birds, not birdies," Charlotte corrected as she shifted in her seat. She kind of wished

Cupcake would sit with her. Snuggling their big dog, with her barrel chest and short tan fur, was always comforting.

"We won't be flying birds around post," Mom added, turning to smile at all three of her kids. "But there's going to be a lot of other really cool stuff."

Though the Baileys had lived in a lot of places, this would be their first time living on post. Mom had explained that the base, which was in Virginia, not too far from Washington, DC, was like a small town, with its own school, snack bar, pool, library, and even a movie theater. And everyone who lived there was either in the army or a military dependent, which even Rosie knew was a family member of someone in the army.

"Is Rex there?" Rosie asked. "Cupcake wants to have a playdate with him."

Rex was a combat dog Mom had met in Afghanistan. She'd sent home a video of the big German shepherd playing Frisbee with his handler during a break, and the whole family had been taken with him.

"No, sweetie, Rex is still working in Afghanistan," Mom said.

"Because he's an MVP dog," Rosie confirmed.

"MWD," Charlotte said, grinning. "Military Working Dog. Though he *was* an MVP in that Frisbee game."

Tom laughed, but Rosie was not amused and gave her sister a sharp look, then turned to Cupcake. "Too bad Rex won't be there," Rosie told their dog. "But I bet you'll make other friends."

"I think that's true," Dad said as he adjusted the sun visor. "All of you guys will make good friends at Fort Patrick." Charlotte noticed him glancing in the rear-view mirror at Rosie when he said this. Her parents had explained to her that Rosie had "issues connecting with her peers." In regular English that meant Rosie wasn't good at making friends, something Charlotte had already noticed because Rosie liked being in charge of everything and often interrupted, two things none of the kids in their neighborhood had liked. Rosie wasn't concerned about this, but Mom and Dad were, signing Rosie up for friendship groups and sessions with the school counselor. So far it had not made a difference, though Charlotte knew her parents were hoping things would change at the post school, which was small and made up of all army kids.

"And we can video chat with Amirah, right?" Rosie asked for what seemed like the millionth time. She wasn't as used to moving around as her older siblings were.

"Absolutely," Mom said. Amirah was the super-nice high school student who had lived two houses down and sometimes babysat for Rosie. "I know you'll want to show her your new room. And Tom can talk to his friends, and Charlotte can call Brynna and Daisy anytime she wants."

"Will we use codes to get into buildings?" Rosie asked, back to her line of questions about life on post.

"No, we'll just use the door," Tom said. "Like regular people."

Apparently Rosie did not care for his tone. "Mom's a spy," she said loftily. "Not regular people." Her eyes narrowed as everyone in the van laughed.

"I'm not exactly a spy, Rosie Posie," Mom said. "I'm military intelligence."

"Tom said that's a spy," Rosie said, arching an eyebrow at her brother.

"I'm in human intelligence, so I do gather information and try to figure out ways to connect to locals when I'm in the field," Mom said diplomatically. "To find the best ways to save army and civilian lives."

"And to find the bad guys, right?" Tom asked.

"Right," Mom confirmed.

Charlotte felt the familiar swell of pride that always blossomed inside her when Mom talked about her work. Lots of moms had cool jobs, but their mom was a major in the US Army, protecting their country, and it didn't get any cooler than that.

"So that means you sneak around and listen in on conversations, like Tom and Charlotte did when they wanted to find out what Mrs. Watkins was hiding in her basement," Rosie said. She smiled sweetly when both her older siblings glared at her.

Mom raised an eyebrow. "Well, my job is kind of the opposite," she said. "I try to connect with people, to make friends, so I can find out how things work on the ground. That information helps our GIs do a better, safer job. But I'm not sure the same can be said for stalking poor Mrs. Watkins." She gave her two older children a pointed look and Charlotte squirmed, gazing down at her hands.

"Rosie's making it sound like a way bigger deal than it was," Tom said quickly. "And it was a lame mission anyway because she just had a bunch of homemade jam down there."

"She gave us some jam on toast," Rosie said, smiling at the memory.

"So it all ended well," Charlotte said hopefully.

Mom gave Charlotte her penetrating stare, the one that always made Charlotte feel like Mom could read every thought swimming around in her brain. "I'll let this one go," Mom said finally. "But no sneaking around Fort Patrick. You need to stay away from the buildings that are off-limits to civilians."

"Do they have some kind of top secret military stuff in them?" Tom asked, leaning forward eagerly.

Charlotte was leaning forward too, despite herself. The situation with Mrs. Watkins had actually been a bit of a mess. In the end, Tom and Charlotte offered to mow her lawn for most of August so she wouldn't rat them out. After that, Charlotte, who had been the one to formulate their failed plan of action, had vowed to hang up her spy shoes forever. But as she considered the possibility of forbidden buildings with top secret things inside, she suddenly wondered if she'd hung them up too soon.

"I don't want to hear anything about the three of

you poking your noses where they don't belong or pestering people with questions," Mom said in the voice that reminded them that she was an officer in the United States Army. "On post we follow the rules, always and no matter what. You guys are going to have a lot more independence living at Fort Patrick, but you need to use that freedom wisely."

Tom gave a whoop and Charlotte couldn't stop grinning. More freedom sounded fantastic. She was about to ask more, but just then the minivan rounded a curve and there, in front of them, was Fort Patrick.

★ CHAPTER 2 ★

As the gates of Fort Patrick came into view, Tom sat up straight and puffed out his chest the tiniest bit. Not that he was the officer in the car—that was Mom. But he *was* a member of an army family and wanted to look like it. He could tell his sisters felt the same way. Charlotte was smoothing back her hair and Rosie was straightening her shirt. Even Cupcake seemed to know something big was happening as she scrambled to her feet and looked out the window.

There were several lanes leading to a security checkpoint that looked kind of like a tollbooth, except for the tower with an armed guard looking down at all the cars. There was also fencing stretching out on either side that was topped with razor wire. No one was getting into Fort Patrick unless they had the clearance to be there. It was kind of like they were driving into a modern-day fortress.

When it was their turn at the booth, Dad passed their IDs to the soldier inside.

"Do they need to do a car inspection too?" Rosie asked eagerly.

"Or look under it with mirrors?" Tom added, remembering some of Mom's stories from living on post in Afghanistan.

But Mom shook her head. "Right now, Fort Patrick is at FPCON Alpha," Mom said. "'Force Protection Condition' is what dictates the level of security getting onto the base, and there aren't mirrors or comprehensive vehicle checks at Alpha. You see that at FPCON Charlie or Delta."

Rosie nodded, clearly tucking the knowledge away for another day when she would probably call it FCFON Alba, Chutney, or Delto.

Once the ID inspection was completed, the soldier handed the cards back and gave Mom a smart salute. Mom may have been assigned instructor duty for the next few years, which was why the family was moving to Fort Patrick, but she could still hit a target from a hundred feet away and wrestle someone twice her size to the ground in under a minute. Mom was the real deal and no one messed with her. Well, except for Rosie, but she was probably going to grow up to be a general.

"Check out the ice cream shop," Charlotte said as they drove slowly down a street lined with stores and restaurants.

"Charlotte, you and Tom are going to be able to walk or bike here whenever you want," Mom said. "Rosie, you'll be able to go with them."

"Really?" Tom asked. In Pennsylvania they'd been able to go around their neighborhood by themselves, but never all the way into town without a grown-up.

"Yup," Mom said. She clicked off the AC, rolled down her window all the way, and rested an elbow on the edge. A warm breeze moved through the car. "You'll be free to go anywhere on post. Anywhere military dependents are permitted, that is," she added.

Tom looked at Charlotte, who was smiling. "That's so cool," she said.

"I think the PX and commissary are that way," Dad said, pointing down a side street. Tom glimpsed the sign for the commissary, the big post grocery shop. The PX was the box store that carried everything from car parts to rain boots. Since Mom worked long hours and Dad had flexibility with his freelance graphic design business, he was the one in charge of household things like shopping, cooking, and the occasional auto repair.

The minivan was now going by the post pool.

"Whoa," Rosie said. Tom gazed out at the waterslides, high dive, and huge stretch of water that made an Olympic-sized pool look like a wading pool. "Whoa" pretty much said it all.

"We can't go swimming alone, can we?" Charlotte asked.

"Actually, you can," Mom said, and Charlotte squealed. "Things on post are safe. Crossing guards will help you get to school, lifeguards are stationed all around the pool, and neighbors here watch out for each other."

Which translated to Tom as even more freedom. This was going to be awesome!

"And here's the residential neighborhood for officers," Mom said as Dad made a right turn. "I think our place is just a few streets away," she went on, peering at numbers on the mailboxes at the end of each drive. As would be expected on an army post, each yard had neatly trimmed grass and carefully tended flower beds without a single weed in sight. The houses themselves were simple ranch style with off-white siding. Tom was hoping maybe their house was a cool color, bright green maybe, but when Dad pulled the minivan into the drive of 32 Bingham Road, the house was the same as the others on the block.

The family piled out and Mom began giving orders. "Tom, you grab those two small duffel bags. Charlotte, the big suitcase is your responsibility, and Rosie, you are in charge of Cupcake."

Rosie and Cupcake ran toward the backyard, both clearly thrilled to finally be out of the car. The front and backyards had fences, which meant Cupcake could roam freely as long as the gate was securely latched. Cupcake would enjoy the yard—she was big on exploring new places, something they all encouraged, because two years ago, when they first met her, Cupcake was a very different dog. Dad and Rosie had heard the sound of crying coming from under a parked car in the lot at the grocery store, peeked under, and seen two terrified brown eyes staring back. It had taken ages to coax the skittish, starving puppy out, and once home, Cupcake had trembled whenever any of them came too close. But lots of food, lots of toys, and above all, lots of love, had transformed Cupcake into the affectionate, playful dog that the Baileys adored.

Tom grabbed a duffel in each hand and headed up the stone path and onto the front porch. It was freshly painted, as were the walls of the entry hall, and the slight scent of lemon cleanser hung in the air.

"There's a nice kitchen," Mom called to Dad, who grinned. He loved cooking and all of the Baileys loved eating his delicious meals.

While Tom was already feeling hungry for dinner—lunch of sandwiches from the cooler felt like a hundred hours ago—he was not concerned with the kitchen just now. His thoughts were on the upstairs, specifically the bedroom situation. Evidently Charlotte was thinking the same thing because she was headed straight for the stairs. Tom tried to cut her off, but Charlotte employed a tricky elbow move and left him in the dust.

Still, he caught up before she'd reached the top of the staircase. They ran down the hall together, investigating each room they came to.

"Dad and I divided up the rooms," Mom said, coming up behind them. She was carrying a garment bag that Tom knew held her army uniform, freshly pressed and ready for action. "Since this house just has three bedrooms, Tom gets the small one and, Charlotte, you and Rosie will have the big one."

Tom sighed. The small room was barely big enough for his bed and desk, plus it was right next to the bathroom. Meanwhile, the big room was *huge*, with built-in bookshelves and three windows.

But Mom was looking at Charlotte sympathetically. "I know we hoped this would be the place you could have your own room, sweetie, but I'm confident you'll make the best of sharing like you always do."

"Rosie's just so messy," Charlotte said, tugging on a braid.

Tom now felt slightly guilty that he was the lucky one with his own room, even if it was small—Rosie really could be a slob.

"If she's messy, she'll fail inspection," Dad said, coming up the stairs and huffing a little from the load of boxes in his arms.

"Rosie's going to have inspection too?" Charlotte asked, surprised. The two older Baileys had been suffering room inspection for years. If Dad, who would have run the cleanest barracks in the entire army, found one thing out of place, allowance was docked. Which was why Charlotte and Tom had the neatest rooms of anyone they knew.

"Dad and I agreed Rosie's old enough," Mom affirmed, leading them into the big bedroom. "And since you two girls are sharing space again, it needs to be livable for both of you."

Dad set a box labeled *Dolls* on the floor. Charlotte loved playing with dolls and had a big dollhouse to go with her collection. Recently she'd starting letting Rosie play with her.

"Okay, I bet it will be fine," Charlotte said with a nod. "As long as she keeps things clean, it will be fun to share the dollhouse in here."

Mom smiled. "That's my girl," she said. Then she headed off to change while Dad walked toward the bathroom with his last two boxes.

Tom was about to ask Charlotte if she wanted to check out the rest of the house, when he heard a sharp sound just outside the window. He jumped straight up, shrieking.

"No need for the screech of doom," Charlotte said calmly. She walked over to the window and looked outside. "It's just acorns falling on the porch roof."

Perhaps it was best Tom didn't have this room after all, if it came with surprise noises. Tom had always had a strong startle reflex, complete with what the family had dubbed the screech of doom. It *was* kind of on the loud side. And very squeaky. Tom kept hoping he'd outgrow it, because screeching was totally mortifying, but it seemed to be hardwired into him, just like his love of comics, his dyslexia, and his aversion to pickles.

Dad poked his head back in the room. "Let's finish unloading the car and do some unpacking while Mom goes in for her meetings."

Tom and Charlotte trooped down the stairs after him, ready to help. But when they got to the front yard, Tom noticed a girl about their age standing in the yard of the house next door, looking over at them.

"Can we go say hi to our neighbor?" Tom asked, hoping to get some tips on post living.

"Sure," Dad said. "Just don't stay out too long. We want to get the house ready so we can enjoy the last few days of summer before school starts."

Tom and Charlotte headed next door.

"Hey," the girl called when they came to the white wooden fence that separated their yards. She had dark brown skin and wore a red headband in her short black curls. "Come on in." She opened the gate for them. "I'm Natasha Wilson, but everyone calls me Tash."

"I'm Tom and this is Charlotte," Tom said.

"Are you guys twins?" Tash asked, looking at them quizzically.

"No, I'm older," Tom said. "But we're both going into sixth grade." It was always good to get the same-grade thing out of the way early on because everyone had questions about it. But to Tom's surprise, Tash just nodded. Tom realized that, as an army kid, she understood about how moving all over the place could end up changing your grade, and he grinned. Living with kids who got army life was going to be awesome.

"I'm going into sixth too," Tash said, frowning slightly. "I hope we don't get too much homework. I play the tuba and I need a lot of time to practice for competitions and stuff."

"Cool," Charlotte said.

Tash smiled. "Yeah, I want to play in a military band when I grow up. And this year at the middle school there's a special band practice that meets before school and sometimes during lunch."

Tom already knew that a number of activities took place during lunch at the Fort Patrick Middle School—that was when he'd be getting his tutoring for dyslexia. He'd been diagnosed in kindergarten, so it wasn't anything new, and at this point all he needed was a good tutor and extra homework time to stay caught up in all his classes. But he didn't feel like thinking about school just yet—not when there were still a few days left of summer.

"So, we were wondering about cool places to—" Tom began, but just then there came a shout from the sidewalk. Tom, Charlotte, and Tash turned to see what was going on.

Two boys were standing in front of Tash's house. One of them, a tall boy with a dark tan and a blond crew cut, was holding a football while the shorter one with sunburned cheeks tried to grab it. Each time his fingers seemed to close around the ball, the taller boy jerked it from his grasp.

"Chase, come on, give it to me," the shorter boy begged. "I need to get home and my dad will kill me if I don't bring that back."

Chase laughed and held the football high above his head. "If you want it, go get it," he said in a taunting tone, and then sent the ball in a whizzing spiral down the street.

The first boy flew after it as Chase followed more slowly, chuckling as he went.

Tom was surprised that the boy, Chase, would just throw a ball like that. What if it had hit an oncoming car and caused an accident?

"That was mean," Charlotte said as she looked after the boys.

Tom definitely agreed with that—the other boy had seemed genuinely upset.

"Yeah, meet Chase Hammond," Tash said with a sigh. "He's in sixth with us, and I'd stay clear of him if I were you guys."

That seemed like excellent advice to Tom.

"Anyway," Tash said, turning back to look at Tom. "What were you about to ask me?"

"Just about what's fun here," Tom said.

"It's our first time living on post," Charlotte added.

Tash grinned. "You guys are going to love it. Have you seen the pool yet?"

Charlotte was grinning too. "Yeah, we drove by. It looks awesome."

"It is," Tash said. "And did you know movies at the post theater are free?"

"No way," Tom said. He loved movies but always had trouble saving up his allowance.

"Yeah," Tash confirmed. "And they get good stuff. It's not like they're just showing old ones from, like, the 1990s."

This was just getting better and better. Tom was about to ask more when Rosie flew into the yard, Cupcake in hot pursuit. "Dad says come home," Rosie said.

Tom saw Tash have the usual moment of confusion about why a small Asian girl was talking to two white kids about their dad.

"This is our sister, Rosie," Charlotte said.

"I'm adopted from China," Rosie announced grandly. She never noticed the confusion, as far as Tom could tell. She was just proud to be adopted.

"Neat," Tash said.

"I know," Rosie said. Then she turned to her siblings. "We need to get home ASAP or you'll get KT duty."

"It's KP," Tom corrected. "Kitchen Police." In the Bailey home that army term meant cleaning chores, and so while Tom was disappointed not to hear more, he knew it was time to get home.

As they headed back to their yard, Tom was feeling good about things. He had his own room, they were surrounded by army kids just like them, and the base was full of awesome things like the greatest pool ever, free movies—and who knew what else?

So far, life on Fort Patrick seemed pretty perfect to Tom.

★ CHAPTER 3 ★

"I can do that!" Rosie exclaimed before Dad could take all the silverware out of the box. He handed it over to her.

Rosie and Dad were in the kitchen unpacking while Mom, Tom, and Charlotte were out doing boring grocery shopping. Rosie liked helping unpack, she liked having time alone with Dad, and she really liked being in charge of things. Especially things that were fun like stacking up the knives and forks in the red plastic holder. Rosie had the holder in one hand, and now that she had the silverware, she was ready. She put the holder into a drawer, but it wouldn't go in right. She pushed a little harder.

"Hang on, sweetie," Dad said. He was standing on the other side of the wooden island putting away plates.

Rosie knew she could do it herself if he'd just give her a chance. She just needed to get the corner in . . . She began using both hands to wedge the holder inside the drawer.

"Rosie, it doesn't fit in that drawer," Dad said. He sounded tired even though it wasn't even dinnertime yet. "Let's try a different one."

He was right. Rosie pulled at the holder, but it was now jammed. She tugged harder and suddenly the whole drawer came flying out with a loud, splintering crack. Rosie nearly toppled over backward, but Cupcake, who had been lying on the floor, jumped behind her, keeping Rosie upright.

"Thanks, Cupcake," Rosie told the dog, who wagged her short tail at the praise. "Dad, this drawer isn't high quality." That was what Mom had said in their last house when a shelf of books caved in. But Dad just frowned.

"Rosie, I'm not sure the quality of the drawer is the problem," he said quietly.

Uh oh. That meant the problem was Rosie.

"Next time maybe you can be more patient," he added.

Rosie had a lot of trouble with patience—what was the point of doing things slowly?—but she hated that she'd disappointed Dad. "Sorry," she said. "I'll try patience next time."

She didn't promise because she never made a

promise she couldn't keep. But Mom and Dad said trying was important and, sure enough, Dad smiled at her.

"Why don't you let me put the silverware holder in the drawer and then hand you the things to put away?" he asked.

That sounded a lot like Dad being in charge and not Rosie.

"But I want to do it," Rosie pleaded.

"Actually," Dad said, taking the drawer and holder from Rosie. "I have an idea—why don't you and Cupcake go explore the neighborhood a bit, maybe see if you can make some friends?"

Rosie forgot all about the drawer. "We can go, just us?" she asked, not believing something so exciting could be true.

"We get to have some new rules here on post," Dad said. "Because things are very safe here."

"Because the army is watching us?" Rosie asked.

"Kind of," Dad said. "They're careful about who gets on post. Plus people here watch out for each other."

"Right," Rosie said, remembering that Mom had talked about this when they arrived. "I know all about that. Okay, see you later."

She was ready to go, but Dad held up a hand.

"Wait, I need to tell you the boundaries," he said.

Rosie sagged, sure the boundaries would ruin everything.

"You can go all the way around our block," Dad said. "No crossing streets, but you'll still see a lot of the residential neighborhood."

"Roger that," Rosie said, and marched to the front door. Cupcake followed.

"I bet you'll run into some kids your age," Dad said, coming up and leaning against the doorjamb as Rosie snapped on Cupcake's leash. "Which would be a good opportunity to make friends. Remember what the counselor said about trying to listen to others and to use kindness, not yelling."

Rosie's mouth pinched up at that. Everyone was worried about her making friends, everyone but Rosie. She had her siblings, she had Cupcake, and she had Mom and Dad—that was more than enough. Maybe kids in her class never wanted to sit with her at lunch or play with her at recess, but Rosie didn't need them anyway. She liked racing around the school yard and climbing up the jungle gym by herself. It was more fun without other kids messing everything up with their bad ideas and complaining when she was in charge.

"I'll look for friends," Rosie told Dad, who began to grin. "Friends for Cupcake. I think she's lonely."

Dad's smile slipped away like soapsuds going down the drain. "I don't think she's the only one who's lonely," he said.

"Right," Rosie agreed. "There's probably another lonely dog out there right now, waiting for a friend just like Cupcake."

Dad sighed. "Okay, well, have fun," he said, then headed back toward the kitchen.

"We get to explore," Rosie told Cupcake, patting the dog on the back of her neck where her fur was thick and satiny. "But you have to listen very carefully to my rules when we go out. I'll be in charge."

Cupcake looked up agreeably as Rosie double-checked that the leash was secure. One of the many wonderful things about Cupcake was that she never minded when Rosie was in charge. In fact, unless she saw a squirrel to chase, she seemed to like it best when Rosie made all the decisions.

Rosie led Cupcake around the boxes stacked up on the porch, then down the steps to the wide side-walk. The sun was bright, and Rosie saw that some of their new neighbors were doing things like mowing their lawns and weeding flower beds. As she considered which way to go, she took a moment to inspect the sidewalk conditions. Their block in Pennsylvania had a big crack right in front of their house, and if you biked over it too fast, your wheel could swerve and you could crash. Rosie had always hated that crack and was pleased to see that the sidewalk pavement here was smooth.

"We'll go this way," Rosie announced to Cupcake. "And find you a friend." Cupcake pranced happily at her side, clearly excited to make friends.

The scent of fresh-cut grass perfumed the air as Rosie and Cupcake made their way around the block.

"Hi there," a woman said. She was pulling up weeds next to her mailbox and wore a floppy straw hat that reminded Rosie of going to the beach. "Welcome to Fort Patrick." She had a Southern accent that made her words sound like music.

"Thanks, ma'am," Rosie said. "I'm Rosie and this is Cupcake."

"I'm Ms. Dunbar," the woman said with a smile. Rosie liked how she didn't seem worried about the dirt all over her hands and clothes. "Are you checking out the neighborhood?"

Rosie nodded. "Yes, and we're looking for friends too."

"There's a lovely boy named Victor who's about your age," Ms. Dunbar said. "He lives in the house across from yours."

"No, not a friend for me," Rosie said. "For Cupcake."

"I see," she said. "Well, good luck."

"Thanks," Rosie said. Ms. Dunbar was way friendlier than grumpy old Mr. Juvais, who had lived next door in their old neighborhood. He was always calling Dad to say that Rosie and her siblings were yelling too loud or riding their bikes too fast. But so far everyone here at Fort Patrick was nice.

Just then Cupcake began to tug on the leash. They had reached the corner, and in the distance Rosie could see the central plaza with the flagpole and the soldier training area beyond. "Cupcake, no, we can't go any farther," Rosie said. "That's the rule. We need to stop here."

Sometimes dogs didn't understand about rules so you had to say it twice. But then Rosie realized Cupcake was trying to sniff the big leafy bush that was below the signpost for Washington Street.

"What's in there, Cupcake?" Rosie asked, worried it might be an escaped prisoner or maybe a wolf that snuck on post, waiting to find someone just the right size to gobble up.

But after a moment a black snout popped out, followed by the rest of a big German shepherd, who walked right up to Cupcake to say hello. Dogs didn't talk in people words, of course, everyone knew that, but Mom had explained that they said hello by sniffing. And it seemed to be a very nice hello from the way both dogs were wagging their tails.

"Cupcake, you found a friend," Rosie said happily, as the two dogs began to romp.

But then Rosie heard someone running toward them and shouting, "Hey! Get away from that dog!"

Rosie turned to see a woman in a blue shirt holding a leash in one hand. She was glowering as she raced up and clipped the German shepherd to the leash, pulling him away from Cupcake.

"No," the woman snapped at Cupcake's new friend. When she turned to Rosie, her expression was angry. Really angry.

"I told you to stay away from this dog," she scolded Rosie, her voice so harsh Cupcake pressed against Rosie's leg.

Rosie was bewildered. "I know about dogs, ma'am,"

she said. "This dog wagged his tail so I could tell he was friendly. And he wants to be friends with my dog, Cupcake. They should have playdates."

"This dog is off-limits," the woman said sharply. Then she jerked at the German shepherd's leash, nearly dragging the dog down the sidewalk.

So it turned out that not everyone at Fort Patrick was nice after all. "That lady was awful," Rosie told Cupcake as she stared after them. "And I don't understand why she wouldn't let that dog play with you."

The worst part of the whole thing was that it had upset Cupcake. Her tail had drooped and her little folded ears were wilted, not perked up and happy like they usually were. Clearly she was miserable at the loss of her friend.

Rosie felt a surge of determination. "Don't worry, Cupcake," she reassured her dog. "We'll find your friend again, I promise."

And she would: Rosie never made a promise she couldn't keep.

★ CHAPTER 4 ★

"Have a good day," Dad called. Tom turned in time to see Dad nearly trip over Cupcake, who had come to the front door to see Tom and Charlotte off on their first day of school. Or to see if they'd dropped any crumbs from the banana muffins Dad had made for breakfast.

"Thanks," Tom said, giving Cupcake a reassuring pat.

"You too, Dad," Charlotte said. Her voice was strained, but that was normal for a first day of school. Tom knew his sister always worried about making friends, and this year, with Tom busy during lunch, Charlotte was particularly stressed about finding people to sit with in the cafeteria. Tom was sure it would all work out though, especially since here on post they were surrounded by kids just like them—army kids.

Tom and Charlotte pulled on their backpacks (green for Tom, purple for Charlotte) while Dad headed back to the kitchen where Rosie was announcing plans to make a hamburger milk shake for Cupcake. Rosie would be going to the elementary school next to the Fort Patrick Middle School, but her day started fifteen minutes later than theirs, so Dad had fifteen minutes to try to talk her out of the milk shake idea.

Tom and Charlotte headed down the front steps. The sun shone brightly and the slight breeze felt good.

"Hey, Baileys," Tash called. She was standing at the foot of their driveway. "Want to walk together?" she asked, tugging on the strap of her pink messenger bag. "I don't start early band practice until next week."

"Sure," Tom said. Maybe walking with a girl who'd been living on post a while would help his sister relax. "So what number school is this for you?" he asked as they started down Bingham Road. Fort Patrick Middle School was only four blocks away.

Tash pursed her lips for a moment as she considered. "We spent two years in Germany and then Hawaii, then Texas, and last year we moved here from DC. So that's five. What about you?"

"We were in Hawaii too, for first and part of second grade," Charlotte said. They stopped at the corner and waited for the crossing guard to wave them across the street. There were barely any cars, but the army clearly made sure the kids were super safe all the way to school. "We lived off post there though, and then we moved to Vermont to be near our grandparents while Mom served in Afghanistan." That had been the hardest two years, barely seeing Mom and worrying every night about whether she would come home at all.

Tash nodded knowingly. "Yeah, Dad was over there for a year, and it was tough," she said.

Again Tom felt the rush of pleasure at being with other kids who knew what army life was really like.

They were almost to the school now and the sidewalk was getting crowded. Two boys shoved past, one of them jostling Tom's arm. He was about to tell the kid to watch it when he realized who it was: Chase Hammond. Which made Tom close his mouth right up.

"That guy really pushes things," Tash said, shaking her head as they walked up the path to the small brick building. "There's no bullying at post schools, but he comes as close to a bully as you get."

Tom would definitely be avoiding Chase, and he wanted to ask Tash why there was no bullying here—that was hard to imagine. But he was distracted by the way Charlotte's face had gone pale as they walked through the metal doors and into the lobby of what looked like any other school: faded cream-colored walls with flyers stating times for band and soccer tryouts, scuffed linoleum floors, and groups of kids standing around and talking. If anything, it was less intimidating than other schools they'd attended because it was so small. Mom had told them there were only fifty sixth graders, which Tom figured would give the school a kind of family feeling. Maybe that was why there was no bullying.

The three of them headed over to the sixth-grade locker alcove. Tom had to spin his combination twice, but then he was able to get it open. The locker smelled like moldy bread, so he quickly stowed his backpack inside and slammed it shut. He and Charlotte had compared schedules the night before and so he knew they were in different homerooms—in fact, they only had one class together all day.

"Good luck, you guys," Tash said, waving as she headed off.

Charlotte was now blinking rapidly, a sure sign she was anxious.

"Don't worry," Tom told her. Really, he didn't get why she was so stressed-out. It was a small school with kids just like them.

But Charlotte still looked pale. "See you later," she said faintly, before heading down the hall to her homeroom.

Sometimes girls were just weird, even his sisters.

Tom walked the other way, checking room numbers until he found 102. He headed inside where about ten other sixth graders were either sitting at desks or standing around talking. A few kids were sitting alone, and Tom wondered if they were new to the base just like him. He sat down next to one of them, a boy wearing an Avengers T-shirt. "Hey, I'm Tom Bailey. We just moved here last week," he said. "Cool shirt."

"Thanks," the boy said. "I'm Kenny Pham. My family's only been here for about three months."

"So who's your favorite Avenger?" Tom asked, ready to discuss one of his all-time favorite topics. But just then the warning bell rang, and someone slipped in right before the teacher shut the door. And when Tom saw who it was, his heart sank: Chase Hammond. Of course, in a school so small, it made sense they'd have some classes together. But it seemed like a bad way to start the day.

"Good morning," their teacher said crisply as he strode toward the front of the room. "I'm Mr. Yanetti, your homeroom teacher as well as your English teacher and social studies teacher. We run a tight ship here at Fort Patrick Middle School, and it starts right here, right now, in my class."

Tom tried not to sigh.

"You raise your hand and you do not speak until you have been called on," Mr. Yanetti said. He had reached the front of the room and was standing in front of the whiteboard, his back straight, his gaze piercing. "This means that if I do not call on you, you do not speak. Should you ignore this rule and speak out of turn, you go to the office. There is no discussion, there are no excuses, it's simply you out the door on your way to chat with Principal Ramirez."

Yikes, this was probably why there was no bullying at a post school: They found the strictest teachers in the universe to teach here.

Mr. Yanetti ran through more rules, did roll call, and then told the class to sit quietly until the bell rang. Tom was scared to breathe too loudly, and he could tell that everyone else felt the same way. Well, everyone except Chase: He was moving restlessly in his seat and yawning loudly enough to earn a look from Mr. Yanetti.

Finally the bell rang, freeing Tom and his classmates. Tom nearly sprinted from the room, hoping that his next class—math with Ms. London—would be better.

But when Tom was almost to the door, a shout in the hall outside made him jump. And when he did, his arm knocked into the boy right behind him.

"Watch it," the boy hissed, and Tom's chest clenched up: Of all the boys he could have elbowed, Tom had elbowed Chase. And somehow when it happened, Chase had dropped something on the ground.

"What's that?" Mr. Yanetti snapped as he marched over to the boys.

Both Tom and Chase took a step back, and there, on the floor, was a small metal object.

"To whom does this belong?" Mr. Yanetti asked, carefully picking it up.

"It's his," Tom said helpfully, pointing at Chase.

He figured Mr. Yanetti would give whatever had fallen back to Chase and that would be the end of it. But instead Mr. Yanetti was scowling and Chase's eyes were wide. And suddenly Tom's heart began to beat just a little bit faster.

"You brought a weapon into school," Mr. Yanetti said to Chase, who sputtered for a moment before managing to speak.

"No, sir, it's not a weapon," Chase said, his voice high and squeaky. "It's just a tiny pocketknife."

Chase and Tom both gazed hopefully at Mr. Yanetti, because this explanation had to make things better. A tiny pocketknife wasn't dangerous after all.

But Mr. Yanetti looked as though Chase had announced it was a microscopic grenade launcher.

"I'll need you to come with me," he said shortly to Chase.

Chase's mouth twisted and he sent Tom a death glare before following their teacher out of the room. After a moment, the rest of the class began to file out. Tom joined them, feeling almost light-headed from all that had gone wrong in such a short amount of time.

"That's not good," Kenny said, coming up to Tom as he headed blindly toward math class.

"I know," Tom said. "But it's not a real weapon, so he won't get in that much trouble, right?"

Kenny's gaze was pitying. "Any kind of weapon in school is bad," he said. "It's definitely big trouble."

Tom didn't get why Kenny said this like it was a death sentence.

"This is a post school," Kenny explained. "And when you get in big trouble at a post school, they don't call your parents."

Tom started to let out a sigh of relief.

"They call your army parent's commanding officer."

Tom's breath caught in his chest. *That* was why there was no bullying. Nothing would be worse than a parent getting scolded by a commanding officer. Nothing.

Well, nothing except Tom's life at Fort Patrick Middle School, now that he had made Chase Hammond his enemy.

CHAPTER 5

The morning had been fine, but the moment of truth was here: It was lunch, and Charlotte was about to walk into the cafeteria. Alone. She took a deep breath as she entered the small buffet area, then instantly regretted it, because the room reeked of overcooked broccoli and greasy burgers, a scent so strong it made her eyes water. Based on that, Charlotte decided to skip the hot lunch line and head over to the sandwich area instead. She debated between turkey and ham but in the end went with cheese and tomato, which would be the easiest on her queasy stomach. She set the cellophane-wrapped sandwich on her tray, then went to the cooler stocked with drinks. She was poking her head in to see if they had any grapefruit juice when a girl came up next to her and reached for a bottle of seltzer.

"I love your nails," the girl said. She had a warm Southern drawl and Charlotte recognized her from both her English and math classes—she was the kind of girl who sparkled a little, radiating confidence, the kind of girl the others crowded around and tried to imitate. The kind of girl who never noticed someone like Charlotte.

Charlotte looked down at her nails, which were painted a minty blue with perfect silver polka dots dancing across them, and smiled shyly. "Thanks," she said.

"I'm Sophia—and you're Charlotte, right?" the girl asked as she headed for the registers to pay. Charlotte followed, surprised Sophia had remembered her name.

"Yeah. My family just moved here last week," Charlotte said. She fumbled for her lunch card.

"Well, welcome," Sophia said, setting her tray on the table by the register and running her fingers through her thick chestnut hair so that her glittery earrings shimmered. Charlotte noticed that she was wearing bronze eye shadow that made her big brown eyes luminous. "And, seriously, your nails are fabulous. Where did you get them done?"

"I did them myself," Charlotte said. She wished she had worn glittery earrings instead of the tiny heart studs she'd put in that morning.

"No way." Sophia grabbed Charlotte's hand to take a closer look.

Charlotte felt her cheeks warm with pleasure. "Yeah, it's kind of a hobby," she said.

"Or a gift," Sophia said, dropping Charlotte's hand and picking up her tray. "Come sit with me and my friend and tell us your tricks."

"Um, okay," Charlotte said, not quite sure how this had happened so easily. Because now she was not walking alone across the cafeteria, humiliated and scared. Instead she was strolling with Sophia, possibly the most popular girl in the class based on the way everyone was greeting her, to sit at her table with her friend. It almost seemed too good to be true.

Sophia led Charlotte to a table that was clearly one of the best: next to a window with a good view of the rest of the large room. Instead of long tables and benches, Fort Patrick Middle School had small square and rectangular Formica tables with seats attached. Charlotte's sneakers squeaked slightly on the scuffed linoleum floor. The smell here was even worse than in the buffet line—it was as though old gym socks had been added to the mix. But Charlotte didn't care about any of that, not when she was being ushered into a seat by Sophia.

"Charlotte, meet Mari," Sophia said, settling down in the chair across from her.

"Hi," Mari said with a friendly smile. Charlotte knew from homeroom that her full name was Mariposa, the Spanish word for butterfly. It fit delicate Mari perfectly, with her long black hair and big brown eyes.

"Welcome to the base," Mari said, spearing some lettuce in her salad. "Where was your family last posted?"

Again Charlotte felt the comfort of being with kids who got army life. "Pennsylvania," she said. "And Vermont before that. But this is our first time living on post."

"Oh, you'll like it," Sophia said. She had a salad too and was drizzling a packet of dressing over it. "You can go shopping without having to wait for your parents to drive you to the mall." Since all three grades ate lunch at the same time, the room rang with voices and laughter so Charlotte had to lean in to hear.

"The PX has everything," Mari affirmed.

"Don't bother buying makeup, though," Sophia said darkly.

"Ms. Ramirez told her there's no makeup in school," Mari said, giving Sophia's arm a sympathetic squeeze.

"Not even lip gloss," Sophia said with a sigh.

"My mom doesn't let me wear makeup," Charlotte said, unwrapping her sandwich, the cellophane crinkling.

"Mine either," Mari said, rolling her eyes. "She still thinks I'm seven. I have to sneak it out of the house in my purse and put it on outside."

"Once she forgot to wash it off before going home," Sophia said, shaking her head. "That was a bad day."

"I bet," Charlotte said. Not that she'd ever snuck out wearing makeup. When your mom was military intelligence, you didn't try to sneak anything. But then something occurred to her. "Wait, is nail polish okay?"

Sophia perked up at that. "Yes, that's okay. Mari, check out Charlotte's nails. They're incredible."

Charlotte's cheeks warmed pleasantly again as she set down her sandwich and held out her hands for Mari to inspect.

"Oh, I love that shade of blue," Mari said, grabbing one of Charlotte's hands to take a closer look. "And those dots are darling. I did stripes on mine." She held out a hand with purple-and-black-striped nails. The stripes were a bit crooked, and Mari frowned at them.

"They're nowhere near as good as yours, though. What's your secret?"

Charlotte grinned. "A bobby pin."

"Brilliant," Sophia proclaimed. The way she said it made Charlotte feel as though she had accomplished something important.

"Hi, Sophia, hi, Mari," a girl said. Charlotte recognized her from science class, though she wasn't sure what her name was. She had shaggy blond hair that she tucked behind one ear as she looked eagerly at Sophia and then at the one empty chair at their table.

"Hi," Sophia said, her voice frosting over slightly as she casually moved her tray so that it blocked the spot. "How's it going?"

The girl took a step back. "Um, good. How was your summer?"

"Nice, thanks," Sophia said. "Maybe we'll see you in class this afternoon."

"Great," the girl said. She held her smile, though the corners of her mouth sagged the littlest bit. "See you."

"Give me a break," Sophia said, rolling her eyes as the girl headed off toward the empty seats where Charlotte had imagined she'd be sitting, the ones near the garbage cans.

Mari was shaking her head. "I can't believe she thought she could sit with us." She turned to Charlotte. "That's Jen Sebastian and she has the worst breath ever."

Charlotte couldn't help snickering at that, though she instantly felt bad.

"And don't get stuck working with her in a small group," Sophia warned. "She just chats the whole time and never does any of the work."

Charlotte knew that talking about people behind their backs wasn't nice. Mom dismissed gossip as small-minded and cruel, while Dad said it was important to remember that one offhand comment could really hurt feelings. But this felt different. First of all, if Jen had bad breath it was a fact, so that shouldn't count as gossip. And second of all, getting advice on who to work with in class was an important part of getting good grades— and good grades mattered in the Bailey home. Plus it wasn't like Jen heard them or knew they were talking about her: She was all the way across the room, at the table by the garbage cans, now chatting with two other girls, no doubt completely happy and oblivious that anyone was saying anything about her. So Charlotte figured it was what Dad called a no harm, no foul situation. And that meant it was okay that she laughed and that she'd probably avoid Jen Sebastian altogether. After all, she wanted to do well at middle school.

"So what are your other manicure tricks?" Sophia asked, smiling at Charlotte like she was the most interesting person in the room.

Charlotte smiled back and leaned forward, ready to talk nails and unable to believe her luck.

CHAPTER 6

"Can we go now?" Rosie asked, and not for the first time.

"I know you're eager to get to the commissary," Dad said, not even looking up from his computer screen. "But like I said before, I need to finish up this project for work first."

"But if we don't go soon we won't have time to get everything ready for the feast," Rosie said anxiously. The Baileys' first day of school feast was an important annual tradition: Dad made his famous spaghetti and meatballs plus buttery garlic bread, they lit candles so everything was fancy, and everyone went around the table saying their goal for the year. Rosie had already put a lot of thought into hers and was ready. And she was also more than ready for her very important job: This year, Dad said she was old enough to be his number-one assistant cooking the feast, which Rosie had been excited about for weeks. But if they didn't get to the commissary soon to buy groceries, the whole thing could be ruined.

"We'll have plenty of time, don't worry," Dad said, his eyes still glued to his computer screen. "Why don't you go upstairs and play with dolls?"

Rosie opened her mouth to explain that dolls were only fun with Charlotte, but Charlotte was still at school, and she didn't know why her school had a half day and the middle school had a regular day, and that was just one more reason Dad needed to be done with his project—

But just then Cupcake butted her head against Rosie's leg and Rosie remembered the other very important thing she needed to do.

"Can Cupcake and I go find Buddy?" she asked, scratching Cupcake on the top of her head, right between her ears the way she loved. Buddy was the name that Rosie had given to Cupcake's friend, the German shepherd who had been snatched away and who Rosie had promised to find.

"Okay, but remember just around the block," Dad reminded, still not looking up.

"I know," Rosie said, already heading toward the front hall for Cupcake's leash.

"Rosie," Dad called. "Remember, if you see any kids from your class, try to strike up a conversation. You never know who might end up being a friend."

This made Rosie scowl, the kind of scowl Mom said was bad manners. But Mom wasn't here and Dad couldn't see her so Rosie scowled as much as she wanted, then marched out. She did not *want* friends; Dad knew that.

The air outside was wet and sweaty, and Rosie's face felt sticky after walking only half a block. A woman was walking toward her on the sidewalk, and Rosie hoped it was Ms. Dunbar since she was so nice. Plus she might know something about Buddy. But as the woman got closer Rosie saw that it was not Ms. Dunbar at all. This woman was older, with painted-on eyebrows and a hat with a saggy silk flower on the brim.

"Hello, ma'am, have you seen a black German shepherd with a big nose?" Rosie asked politely.

"I don't believe so," the woman said. "And aren't you just a little China doll."

Rosie's whole face pinched up tight. This was not the first time someone had called her a China doll, and she did not like it at all. "No, ma'am, you are wrong," Rosie said, careful to remember manners in case this woman was like Mr. Juvais from back in Pennsylvania, who liked to call Mom and Dad to tattle. "I'm not a

China doll. I was born in China and now I'm American, and I'm not like a doll at all."

The woman put a hand on her chest midway through Rosie's statement. "Well, I certainly see that," the woman huffed, her voice full of icicles. Then she walked away.

So far, this afternoon was not off to a good start. But then Rosie looked down at Cupcake, who wagged her tail and licked Rosie's hand. "Don't worry," Rosie told Cupcake. "We're going to find your friend." That would make everything better.

"Hi, Rosie."

Rosie spun around when she heard her name, hoping maybe it was Charlotte or Tom home early. Unfortunately, though, the soft voice had come from a quiet boy Rosie recognized from her class, whose eyes were red and watery like the sick hippo in a book Dad once read to Rosie. Rosie did not like sick hippos.

"What do you want?" Rosie asked.

The boy seemed to shrink into his baggy red T-shirt. "I'm Victor. From your class. Do you want to play?" he nearly whispered.

"No thank you," she said. "I'm busy looking for something."

"What are you trying to find?" Victor asked eagerly.

"It's none of your concern," Rosie told Victor in a lofty tone. She turned and started down the sidewalk.

"Maybe I can help," Victor said, trailing after Rosie.

This was why Rosie didn't want friends: They said they wanted to play too, but then they tried to be in charge or change the rules. Finding Buddy was Rosie's project, and she didn't need Victor trying to take over. "No," she said firmly.

The red in Victor's eyes got just a little redder, and Rosie felt a twinge of guilt. But really it was his own fault for not listening in the first place. Rosie was on a mission to find Buddy, and this quiet boy would only slow things down. So Rosie very politely waved good-bye to Victor and headed around the block, stopping at each house and peering into every yard.

But hard as she looked, she never found any sign of the black-nosed German shepherd.

"Okay, let's hear everyone's goals for the year," Mom said. The Baileys were gathered around the big wooden table that had moved with them to every new home in every new place they had ever lived. It was sturdy and the edges had softened with time. Before it belonged to Rosie and her family, it had belonged to Dad's family when he was a little boy, and to Grandma Bailey's family when she was a little girl. Which made it really super old. Some nights Rosie liked running her fingers softly over the worn spot near her place mat, where she imagined Dad might have rubbed his fingers back when he was a boy who read comics and ran around just like Rosie.

"Tom, start us off," Mom said, looking at Tom over her glass as she took a sip of sparkling cider.

Tom was twining spaghetti around and around his fork, but he let it slither off when Mom spoke to him. "Um, I guess my goal is to keep working on my reading, to stay caught up and everything," he said.

Mom nodded. "Did you meet your tutor today?" she asked.

Tom looked slightly more cheerful. "Yeah, at lunch, and she's really nice," he said. "I think it's going to be good working with her."

"I'm glad to hear it," Mom said.

"Can I go next?" Charlotte asked in a bubbly voice.

"Sure," Mom said, smiling at her.

"So, I definitely want to do well in all my classes," Charlotte said. "Even science, where we have to dissect a worm."

"Gross," Rosie said, crinkling her nose.

Charlotte smiled at her. "Tell me about it," she said. "And I also want to make new friends."

Dad nodded approvingly. "That's a good set of goals," he said. "And it sounds like you already met some kids you like."

"Yeah, they're great," Charlotte said, beaming and reaching for another slice of garlic bread.

"Are they like Brynna and Daisy?" Rosie asked. Charlotte's friends from Pennsylvania had always included her the times they came over to play dolls and bake cookies.

Charlotte bit her lip for a moment, then shook her head. "Not really," she said.

"They'd better be nice if they come over to play dolls," Rosie said, already worried at the thought of being left out. Not that Charlotte had friends over often—the Baileys usually spent weekends together. But if she did, Rosie would definitely need to be included.

"Um, I don't think they'll come over to play dolls," Charlotte said.

"But they're nice, right?" Mom asked, tilting her head slightly as she looked at Charlotte.

"Totally," Charlotte said quickly. "And it's really cool to hang out with other girls who get what it's like to live in a military family."

Rosie nodded. That made sense. She still felt wary of these friends, though.

"Did you find that too, Tom?" Mom asked.

Tom paused for a fraction of a second. "Yeah, it's good," he said.

"Is everything okay?" Mom asked, setting down her fork.

"It's fine," he said. "Just adjusting to a new school." He finally ate a bite of spaghetti.

Mom narrowed her eyes slightly, but then let out a breath and turned to Rosie. "How about you, Rosie Posie?" she asked with a big smile. "What's your goal for the year?"

Rosie smiled back. She had thought about her goal very carefully and had picked out something extra good.

But before she could reply, Dad butted in. "You know, a wonderful goal would be making friends," he said.

Mom nodded. "True, that's a great thing to strive for."

Rosie slumped down in her seat. That was not her goal at all, and she did not like how her parents kept bringing it up.

"Okay, well, why don't you tell us the goal you chose," Dad said, but Rosie could tell he wanted her to use his.

"My goal is to be Student of the Week," Rosie said. "Because Student of the Week gets to feed Isabelle the Iguana."

Mom nodded. "That's a lovely goal," she said.

It was, though Rosie was not sure Mom actually meant it. In fact, Rosie had a sneaking suspicion that Mom thought feeding Isabelle was not as good as making friends.

"I have an important announcement," Dad said.

Rosie looked up, hoping the announcement involved a trip to the post ice cream parlor.

"Today's dinner would not have been possible without help from my new assistant, Rosie," Dad said.

Rosie sat up straight and tall at that.

"Rosie Posie, you've also been very responsible walking Cupcake and cleaning up your room," Mom added, and Charlotte nodded, giving Rosie a thumbs-up. "You've passed inspection every day this week."

Now Rosie was beaming as a cozy warmth wrapped around her like a snuggly blanket.

"Here's to the first day of school," Mom said, lifting her glass up in a toast. "And all of us reaching our goals."

Rosie stood up, now convinced that this was the best first day feast ever. "Roger that!" she cried.

"Roger that!" her siblings echoed, as all five Baileys clinked glasses in honor of the new school year.

CHAPTER 7

One of the things Tom liked about having a military mom was hearing about the tactics, strategy, and vast number of elements that went into planning any intelligence mission.

When Mom did her tour in Afghanistan, the family had learned about being an operative in a hostile environment. Mom's letters described some of the methods she and her team used when carrying out a clandestine operation, like using camouflage to move unnoticed and concealment to hide and evade being detected by the enemy. But that information had never felt relevant to Tom's own life until the terrible pocketknife incident with Chase.

Now, on Friday morning, as Tom skulked down the hall of Fort Patrick Middle School feeling vulnerable to attack at any moment, he realized that *he* was an operative in a hostile environment. And if he wanted to survive the rest of the day, let alone the rest of the year, he was going to need some new tactics.

Three days of Chase shoving Tom whenever he passed, sneering at him, and making rude comments under his breath had made that all too clear. What made matters even worse was that the other boys in the class saw all of this, and no one wanted any part of it, which meant Tom was completely on his own in enemy territory. Yesterday afternoon had been the worst so far—Chase elbowed Tom in the back while he stood at his locker, and Tom had hit his face on the sharp edge of the locker door. He had also nearly screeched at the surprise attack, but bit his tongue in time. But Tom knew his luck was running out fast. It was time to make a plan of action.

As Tom made his way through the crowded hall, he thought he heard Chase up ahead. Just in case, he quickly turned back around, happy to take the long way to class if it meant avoiding Chase. But he knew he couldn't just run from Chase all year—that wouldn't be feasible, plus it would mean Tom would have a new problem of being tardy to class. Tom bent over a water fountain, his face hidden, and considered other options.

The best goal would probably be trying to redirect Chase. Tom could use Mom's methods of camouflage and concealment to hide himself in plain sight, so that

Chase stopped noticing him and found another target. Which wasn't all that farfetched—after three days of dealing with Chase, Tom knew what a short fuse he had and how easy it was for that fuse to ignite. If Tom could just stay out of Chase's crosshairs until Chase identified a new target, Tom would be home free.

In the past Tom would have relied on Charlotte to be part of his mission, because as Mom always said, you wanted someone to have your back at all times. But because they had so many different classes, because Tom didn't have lunch in the cafeteria, and mostly because Charlotte was consumed with her new friends, she hadn't even noticed what was happening. And Tom was too ashamed to tell her. He was the big brother after all. And so as he headed toward his English class with his head down, shoulders hunched, ducking behind bigger kids whenever possible, Tom was working solo.

Dad often said Mom was good at treading lightly, which gave her the advantage of being able to spot an enemy before the enemy spotted her. Tom tried to emulate that as he slipped into the classroom, the worst class of the day because he was actually seated next to Chase. Tom did a quick scan of the room and saw that he had arrived before Chase. Good. He walked carefully and quietly to his seat, then slid down to make himself as small as possible. It wasn't as good as actual camouflage of course, but hopefully it would still do the trick.

"Hey, Tom," Kenny said from across the aisle. He waved the new *Hulk* comic at Tom—one Tom would normally be excited to check out.

But Tom just gave a quick nod, then turned away and ducked down even lower in preparation for Chase's arrival. He didn't need Kenny attracting attention his way.

Chase came in as the bell rang and Mr. Yanetti was closing the door. Tom kept his focus down on his desk, but from the corner of his eye he could see Chase settle into his seat and begin unpacking his supplies for the class. He didn't seem to register Tom at all.

Tom let out a small breath of relief. The fact that Chase hadn't muttered anything or even glared at him had to be a sign that Tom's mission was off to a good start.

"All right, everybody, take out your homework from last night and set it on your desk," Mr. Yanetti said. "I'll come around and collect it." Even his most basic commands sounded like orders, and Tom, along with the rest of the class, moved fast.

Tom had spent over an hour on the short-answer reading questions, and now he gently removed the two pages from his binder, being careful not to wrinkle them. Mr. Yanetti, who had been assigning homework since the first day of school, had a policy that all work needed to be neat and legible or it would have to be redone. Tom smoothed his papers, feeling a flicker of pride at how good they looked. Maybe he hadn't made any friends at school, but at least he'd get a good grade on this assignment.

And then, suddenly, several wet black blobs appeared on Tom pages, bleeding into big splotches that obliterated Tom's work. "Hey!" he shouted, the word brittle and loud as he whipped his head around to see what could have caused such a disaster.

When he caught Chase's eye, he knew. Chase was smirking and for a quick second he flashed the tiny sprayer he'd used to send colored water splashing right onto Tom's paper. Of course Chase had perfect aim.

"Why is there yelling?" Mr. Yanetti asked sharply, turning around from where he'd been collecting papers at the far end of the room.

"He ruined my homework," Tom said, possibly a bit too loudly. But his heart was beating hard and he was

almost panting, as if the ink had been a weapon someone had just used in a surprise attack. Which it actually
kind of was. Tom's hand was shaking as he held up the
soggy pages to show the teacher, certain Mr. Yanetti
would be as upset as Tom.

"Bailey, you need to take responsibility for your
own work," Mr. Yanetti said. "We don't blame other
people for our mistakes, not in this class."

"But, sir—" Tom protested.

"You can redo the assignment for half credit," Mr.
Yanetti said. He was back to collecting homework from
the other students.

"Wait, why would I only get half credit for the work,
sir?" Tom asked. He must have misunderstood. And it
would take him another hour to remember all his
answers since the pages were now completely illegible.

"I am offering you half credit to give you a chance to
correct your mistake," Mr. Yanetti said.

"But this isn't fair, and he—" Tom started.

Mr. Yanetti turned to glare at Tom, who crumpled
under the harshness of his gaze.

"Sorry, sir," Tom whispered. Tears of fury and
frustration pricked his eyes and he blinked them
away fast.

He heard the slightest snicker and looked over to see Chase, who was grinning. "You had it coming," he whispered.

But Chase had pushed his luck just a little too far. "Are you speaking out of turn in my class?" Mr. Yanetti asked, his sharp gaze falling on Chase.

"Sorry, sir," Chase said. Tom could hear a scratchy hint of anger in his voice.

"Both of you boys have detention," Mr. Yanetti said. "Right now that's just for the next two weeks, but if I hear a single word out of either of you, if you so much as breathe loudly, that turns into a month. Are we clear?"

"Yes, sir," Tom and Chase both mumbled.

Chase was looking at Tom again and this time he was not smiling. With sickening certainty Tom knew that the fallout from this disastrous mission would be bad. Really bad.

Detention was awful, of course. Mr. Yanetti sat at his desk at the front of the room, watching them the whole time. He insisted on complete silence from Tom, Chase, and a girl named Simone who'd had the misfortune of getting caught passing a note in Mr. Yanetti's other English class. Simone's eyes were teary and she sniffled the whole forty minutes, making Tom even more miserable. When Mr. Yanetti finally dismissed them, Tom was beyond eager to get home. Still, he sat and waited for Chase to leave first. He did not want to have another run-in with his enemy, not today.

So Tom left the building last, grabbed his bike, which he'd ridden to school with Charlotte this morning, and headed home, his shoulders slumped under the weight of his backpack and the worries he carried with him. It was another muggy afternoon and his T-shirt was damp and unpleasantly sticky under the nylon backpack by the time he reached Bingham Road. He waved to several neighbors who were outside gardening, then coasted down the sidewalk and was about to turn onto his block when something hit him.

Tom let out an epic screech of doom.

Blinded by a powerful stream of water, he swerved directly into a tree. He fell off his bike, choking from the water that had gotten into his mouth and hoping that it had muffled the screech. Because when he finally wiped off his face enough to see what had happened, he saw Chase, a hose in one hand, his phone in the other, laughing his head off.

"Very funny," Tom said, trying to sound dismissive. But his voice was wobbly, he was still kneeling in the grass, and he was wet and bedraggled from the spray.

"It *was* funny," Chase agreed, dropping the hose so he could wipe his eyes too. Though in his case he was swiping away tears of laughter. "Man, you're a real wimp, screaming like that over a little bit of water."

It had been more than just a little bit of water and it had hit Tom hard, but he knew there was no way to say that and not sound like an even bigger wimp. So he stood silent and sopping, unable to think of a way to defend himself at all.

"My dad's going to be pretty angry about that detention," Chase said. "So I wanted to find a way to thank you for it." His eyes were glinting, like a snake inspecting its prey before going in for the deathblow. "I'm just glad I got a photo of it"—he held up his phone—"so everyone else at school can see it too."

Tom's knees were weak. Once his classmates saw that, he'd be a complete laughingstock.

But Chase wasn't done with him yet. "See you Monday, Sergeant Wimpy," Chase said, grinning at his new name for Tom.

There it was, the deathblow. Because Tom knew, no matter how he plotted or strategized, no mission in the world could save him from his fate now.

Blinking back tears, Tom grabbed his bike and took off, away from home so he wouldn't have to face his family wet and humiliated. At the edge of their neighborhood he turned left down Washington Street, passing the park and rec center and then the pool. At Patrick Boulevard he turned right, heading toward the woods and the lake beyond. It wasn't that he wanted to go to the lake, really; he just wanted to go where there weren't kids or neighbors or anyone else, just the road in front of him and the wind at his back. The trees shaded him as he rode, only a few cars passing and all of them careful to give him a wide berth. Sweat ran down his back, or maybe it was water from the drenching he'd received. Either way it made his skin crawl. When he reached the boathouse he didn't stop but instead went in a wide circle and headed back to the main part of post.

But then at Crimson Drive, when Tom stopped at the traffic light, he realized he wasn't ready to go home, not yet. So he turned right, riding along Crimson Drive until he reached a road so narrow he nearly passed it. And as he looked down the small tree-lined street, he felt something other than misery: curiosity. Because on a base alive with activity at all times, this little alley seemed completely remote. So Tom pedaled over to check it out.

There was only one building on the quiet, wooded one-way road. It was a large wooden structure with two floors and a big yard out front that wasn't exactly sloppy—this was an army base after all—but it wasn't as neatly kept up as the area around the other buildings on post. The bushes grew a bit higher, and it had been a little while since the lawn had been mowed. There were no cars in the driveway, and the trees close to the building shaded it so completely that no sunlight fell over the house or the yard. The windows were dark and several on the second floor were boarded up.

Tom was even more curious now, so he parked his bike at the end of the drive and approached the building. The air was still and it was quiet—no birds flew overhead and no little animals scuttled through the yard. Tom slowed as he reached the steps to the front porch. Despite the heat of the day it felt chilly, perhaps from the thick cover of trees above. And then Tom saw a slight movement through one of the panes of glass in a small side window, a flicker as though someone or something had walked past. Goose bumps prickled his arms.

A sound came from inside the house, a moan so faint Tom wasn't sure if maybe he was just imagining it. But after a moment it came again and Tom jerked back, picturing a zombie or banshee wailing as it clawed its way across the basement floor toward him.

Just then Tom felt a sharp tap on his shoulder. He leaped in the air, screeching the screech of doom, then turned and saw a soldier, sweaty in his fatigues and not the least bit zombie-like or scary.

"You okay?" the soldier asked. He was looking at Tom with concern. "Sorry to startle you. But this is a restricted area. You need to move along."

Tom did not need to be asked twice. Whatever was inside that building had him completely spooked, and he was not sorry to leave it behind as he hopped on his bike and pedaled away.

But as Tom biked through the central plaza, stopping to let a line of soldiers marching in formation pass, the ugly name Chase had called him came back to him. *Sergeant Wimpy.* And Tom couldn't help but wonder if maybe, just maybe, the name fit.

CHAPTER 8

Help!!!

Charlotte looked down at the text that had just arrived on her phone, then grinned.

What can I do? she typed quickly to Sophia, then leaned back in her desk chair waiting for a reply. After a brunch of Dad's blueberry pancakes and sausage, she and Tom had headed upstairs to take care of their homework, a Saturday routine in the Bailey home. Charlotte was almost done with math, which was her last assignment, and welcomed a break, especially one that involved her new friend.

Advice needed, came Sophia's reply and a moment later a photo followed. Charlotte carefully examined the shot of Sophia's nails. She was clearly trying to do gold stripes on her rose-colored nails, but they were uneven with raggedy edges.

The answer you seek is tape, Charlotte typed, then paused before sending it. That was the way she joked around with her siblings, but it sounded kind of babyish, kind of like the dollhouse she planned to hide if Sophia and Mari ever came over. She deleted the text and started again. **Use tape**, she wrote instead.

You're a genius!!!! came the reply, followed by a string of excited emojis.

That made Charlotte's grin even wider, though she wasn't quite sure how to respond. She couldn't say thank you to something that was obviously half a joke, but then what should she say? After considering for a moment, she sent back her own string of emojis, including her two favorites, a jaunty snowman and a scarlet poppy, and hoped that was all right.

Got to go with my mom to the px but come to the pool tmrw, Sophia wrote.

Will try, Charlotte texted back. The words were casual, but Charlotte's insides were delightfully fizzy from the invitation and the whole exchange. Being friends with Sophia and Mari was so much fun! Of course Charlotte had liked Brynna and Daisy back in Pennsylvania, and her friend Ella in Vermont before that. But they were girls like Charlotte, the kind of girls who sat near the garbage cans in the cafeteria, who talked about homework and their hobbies, and who passed through the halls unnoticed. Which was fine, perfectly fine. But it wasn't exciting, not like Sophia and Mari, who sat at the best table in the cafeteria, who made funny jokes about classmates, and who couldn't walk two feet down the hall without people calling to them, wanting to see and be seen with them. Charlotte was a part of that now, a girl people noticed. Even though she was new, everyone already knew who she was. And she liked it more than she ever would have dreamed.

"Are you done with your homework yet?" Rosie asked.

Charlotte startled slightly—she hadn't heard her sister come in.

"Pretty much," she said, stretching a little and then standing up. The math would only take another ten minutes—she could finish it later.

Cupcake, who had been dozing in a sunny spot on the rug, ran over to greet Charlotte and Rosie as though she hadn't seen either of them in weeks.

"Dad says we can go explore," Rosie said. She bent down to cuddle Cupcake and the big dog wriggled with joy, her short tail wagging furiously.

"Sounds good," Charlotte agreed. She reached over to scratch Cupcake between her ears the way she loved.

Cupcake rewarded her with an affectionate lick on the hand.

"Cupcake's lonely," Rosie said. "She needs me to find Buddy."

Charlotte tried not to sigh at this, at least not out loud.

"Don't worry, Cupcake," Rosie crooned to the dog, who looked perfectly happy to Charlotte. "I promised I'd find your friend and I will."

"Want to get going?" Charlotte asked, standing up. It would be fun to check out more of the base.

"Okay," Rosie said. "Let's get Tom."

Charlotte followed her sister out of the room, wondering how Tom would react. Normally she'd assume he would be as eager as she and Rosie were, but he'd been weird the past few days, quiet and distracted, but denying anything was wrong when Charlotte asked.

And when they walked into his room he wasn't even working—he was just sitting at his desk staring into space.

"Tom, we're going biking around the post," Rosie announced, brushing her bangs out of her face. "And everyone needs to make sure to look for Buddy," she added.

Charlotte was seriously getting tired of hearing about this dog Rosie was so worked up about. She was sure Cupcake was just fine without this new friend. Tom had to be as impatient with the whole Buddy thing as she was, but he didn't seem to have even heard. Cupcake nuzzled his hand and he patted her absently.

"Hurry up," Rosie said cheerfully.

Tom cleared his throat, then stood up. "Okay," he said, but his voice sounded far away.

"Are you all right?" Charlotte asked for possibly the hundredth time since the first day of school.

And for the hundredth time Tom nodded mechanically. "Yeah, fine," he said.

Charlotte bit her lip as she looked at her brother. What was he keeping from them? And why? Tom was never one for secrets; none of the Baileys were. But Tom was clearly holding *something* back as he brushed past, not meeting her eyes.

Charlotte sighed, then went after him.

After saying good-bye to Dad and Cupcake, the three siblings grabbed their bikes from the garage and pedaled down Bingham Road, heading toward the main plaza. They stopped at a light on Washington Street and Patrick Boulevard.

"Should we turn here or keep going?" Charlotte asked. All directions seemed promising since the base was hopping with activity.

"Keep going," Rosie decided.

They waited for several army jeeps and a civilian car to pass, then rode toward Gettysburg Drive. Charlotte was in the lead and she didn't stop until they'd reached the obstacle course next to the big training field on Adams Drive.

"Who do you think is going to win?" Charlotte asked her siblings as they pulled up next to her. A platoon was coming to the end of the course, all of them dripping sweat as they raced to be the first one done.

"I think that woman is the best," Rosie said, pointing at the soldier leaping over a pit of mud before landing gracefully, securing her weapon, and lowering to her belly to shimmy under a maze of razor wire.

"Yeah, she's good," Tom agreed.

The other members of the soldier's platoon were close behind, but she was clearly in the lead. Their sergeant, whistle in hand, supervised.

"She's almost as strong as Mom," Charlotte said, shielding her eyes from the bright sun as she watched the soldiers climbing up and over a wooden wall. She was hot and sticky just standing there watching—the soldiers must be sweltering, yet none of them slowed.

They watched as the sergeant ordered the last soldier over the wall to drop and do twenty push-ups. "Can Mom make people do that?" Rosie asked.

Charlotte smiled. "I don't think so," she said. "Mom works in the Military Intelligence Training office, and I don't think they have people do push-ups there."

Rosie brushed a stray lock of black hair back from her face and crinkled her nose. "That's boring," she said.

"Teaching people how to be super-spies and stop the bad guys is not boring," Charlotte pointed out.

Rosie considered this and then nodded. "I'm thirsty," she announced. "Can we get juice?"

"Sure," Charlotte agreed. Her lips were dry and a cold drink sounded great.

The Baileys got back on their bikes, and Tom led the way down Adams Drive. They passed several administrative buildings, an indoor training center, and a group of soldiers marching in crisp formation across a wide green field. The sun beat down as they passed the barracks where new recruits lived and the mess hall next door.

"We should get library cards," Charlotte called as they passed the big brick library on the corner.

"Roger that," Rosie called back.

They turned on Patrick Boulevard, passing the movie theater and a pizza shop before coming to a stop in front of the small deli that sold newspapers and snacks.

The chill of air-conditioning wrapped around them as they stepped inside the store, cool and delicious after the sun.

"Are you getting yucky grapefruit?" Rosie asked. She was reaching for a bottle of apple juice.

"Definitely," Charlotte said. She knew it was strange, but she loved the way it made her lips pucker and quenched her thirst on a hot day like nothing else ever could. She was pleased to see a row of fresh-squeezed juice and selected a container of pink grapefruit, slick with condensation.

"Ready?" Tom asked. He was already up at the register with his lemonade and handing the clerk their money. Charlotte took a gulp of her juice and then followed her siblings to the door.

Outside Charlotte saw Tash coming out of the café across the street with her mom. When Tash spotted the Baileys, she headed over.

"Hey," Tash said. She was wearing cutoffs and a green T-shirt dotted with musical notes.

"We're exploring the post," Rosie told Tash importantly.

Tash smiled at her. "Find anything fun?"

"We watched some GIs on the obstacle course," Rosie said. "Someday I want to try that."

"Me too," Tash agreed. "Though it looks kind of scary."

Rosie snorted. "That's not scary at all."

Charlotte laughed. "It takes more than a wall and some razor wire to spook Rosie," she said, swigging on her nearly empty juice bottle.

Tash's eyes lit up. "Oh, I know what might do it," she said. "Have you guys heard about the haunted house on the alley off Crimson Drive?"

Rosie's eyes got big. "No," she said. "Tell us."

Charlotte smiled, impressed that Tash was so good with Rosie. And needless to say she was interested in the haunted house too.

"It's this old abandoned building, all dark and dingy, with spiderwebs and boarded-up windows," Tash began, lowering her voice. "None of the adults will talk about it—they just tell you to stay away and not to ask questions."

With a start Charlotte realized that was exactly what Mom had said about the restricted buildings on post.

"But all the kids on post know that years ago the army used to do experiments there," Tash went on. "Top secret experiments."

"What were they trying to do?" Rosie asked breathlessly.

"The story goes that they were trying to create some kind of super-soldier," Tash said. "And then it all went wrong, and they had to close it up really fast. All the doctors working on the project just kind of disappeared."

"What about the soldiers they were experimenting on?" Charlotte asked, so caught up in the story she nearly shivered despite the heat of the day.

"That's the thing," Tash said. "Some of them never made it out."

"So they're still trapped in there?" Rosie asked, clearly rapt.

"People even say some of them might have died in there," Tash said.

"So now they're ghosts," Rosie whispered.

Any normal six-year-old would find that a scary prospect, but Rosie just looked excited to find out more.

"No one knows for sure," Tash said. "But bad things happen when you get near that building. If you get too close, you hear noises like—"

"Like moans," Tom said.

"Exactly," Tash said, and they all turned to look at him.

"How do you know that?" Rosie asked.

"I biked by there the other day," Tom said. "I didn't know what it was, but it looked interesting so I stopped."

"You went exploring without us?" Charlotte asked, her voice suddenly squeaky, her feelings about to be very hurt if Tom said yes. The Baileys always explored cool new places as a team. Always.

Tom had an odd look on his face, almost like he was embarrassed. "No, I didn't get close or anything. I . . . I wanted to wait for you guys."

Charlotte let out a breath—that was okay, then— he'd waited for them before getting to the fun part.

"Anyway," Tom went on, "as I was leaving, a GI came and told me the whole place is off-limits."

Tash nodded. "Yup, that's what they say, but—" She broke off suddenly as her mom came up.

"Hi, Baileys," Mrs. Wilson said cheerfully. "Tash, are

you ready? I know you want to get in some practice time before dinner."

"Right," Tash said, turning so she could give the Baileys a knowing look before heading off with her mom.

"Do you think that house is really haunted?" Rosie asked eagerly.

"I'm not sure," Charlotte said. "But there's only one way to find out—let's go see it." Charlotte wasn't sure she believed in ghosts, but Tash's story was pretty convincing. Charlotte definitely wanted to check out the house for herself and see what was really going on there. And judging from the gleeful expression on Rosie's face, Charlotte knew her sister felt exactly the same way.

But Tom bit his lip. He seemed about to say something when the sound of a bugle rang out of the post loudspeaker. The cars driving down Patrick Boulevard came to a halt, and the drivers stepped out of their vehicles. Everyone on the street paused and turned toward the flag that waved in the distance at the central plaza of the post.

"It's 'Retreat,'" Charlotte whispered to Rosie. Her sister nodded, her eyes wide. Though they had heard faint bugle sounds before, this was their first time being near enough to the central square to see it firsthand. The three of them stood still as the song played and then placed their hands on their hearts as "To the Colors" came next, the flag lowering slowly into the hands of a waiting soldier as the last notes shimmered in the air. Then the soldiers on the field went back to training, the drivers got back in their cars, and the normal events of the day resumed.

"That's so cool," Rosie said, her eyes still wide.

"I know," Charlotte agreed. The whole thing had given her shivers. Mom said that even after all her years of "Retreat" in the evening, "Reveille" in the morning, and "Taps" late at night, she still got chills every time she stopped and took a few minutes to honor the flag.

Tom looked relieved. "That means it's five," he said. "We'd better head home."

He tossed his empty bottle in the recycle bin on the corner, and his sisters did the same.

Charlotte hadn't realized it was so late, but Dad had said to be back before five thirty. "Yeah, I guess this means we'll live to see another day," she said with a grin.

Rosie laughed, but as they climbed back on their bikes and headed for home, Charlotte realized that Tom had not even cracked a smile.

CHAPTER 9

"It's my turn," Rosie said fiercely to the girl from her class who was trying to cut the line. Rosie had been waiting for a million hours to go down the water slide at the Fort Patrick pool, and she wasn't going to wait a second longer than necessary.

When she'd woken up that morning, the sun was bright, the sky was clear, and Dad had said he'd take them to the pool. Rosie, who had been waiting since that first day to dip her toes into the waters of the best pool she'd ever seen, had been overjoyed, and the pool had not disappointed. It was huge, with a special soaker area with showers that sprayed swimmers, four different diving boards, and two slides—one for little kids, and this one: the big twisty slide that whooshed you out with a huge splash into the deep section of the pool. Rosie had already done it once and she couldn't wait to go again, this time face-first. Which was why she was angry at Aisha for trying to cut.

"Oh, sorry," Aisha said, shrinking back a little at

Rosie's tone. It was only then that Rosie realized it was just a mistake and Aisha hadn't meant to cut. But then Aisha turned to her friend Oscar who was standing behind them. "That girl is mean," she whispered.

"No one wants to be friends with her," Oscar agreed.

Rosie whirled around to tell them that she didn't want to be friends with them or anyone else in her class anyway, but then a big kid in line behind them spoke up. "Are you going down the slide or did you chicken out?" he asked Rosie.

"I never chicken out," Rosie cried, stung by the accusation. She grabbed her mat and practically threw herself down the slide. The wind whipped in her hair as she picked up speed, flying around one turn and then getting to the twisty part where water sprayed in her face. She shrieked with delight when she finally went barreling into the pool, the water deliciously cool.

But as she wiped the water from her eyes and gathered up her mat, there was a muddy feeling in her belly from the things Aisha and Oscar had said. Rosie hadn't tried to be rude—she just didn't want anyone cutting in front of her. But now Aisha thought she was mean, and Oscar did too. Plus they probably remembered how on Friday at school Rosie had yelled at Benny for taking too long on the swings and at Debbi for hogging all the markers during art.

Rosie's shoulders slumped. She really didn't think it was her fault, though—they shouldn't have been so pushy in the first place. And Aisha should be more careful if she didn't want people getting upset at her for cutting.

Rosie pulled herself out of the pool, set her mat on the pile next to the slide, and started toward the diving board. The chlorine smell and sounds of little kids squealing with happiness, older kids talking and laughing, and the general festive feel of the pool started to lift her spirits a bit. Maybe she'd do a cannonball from the highest diving board, even though it was almost as tall as a skyscraper. That would be amazing. She started to smile again, just thinking about it.

"Hey, Rosie Posie, you looked great on the slide," Dad said, walking up to her. He'd been sitting in the family area, a big grassy section where everyone spread out towels. Lots of grown-ups sat there and chatted or read while kids swam, which Rosie did not understand. It was burning hot, so the place to be was in the pool, not next to it.

"Yeah, it was really Bravo Zippy," Rosie said, happy to see Dad, even though he was wearing a big straw hat that looked kind of silly.

Dad smiled. "I think it's Bravo Zulu, for good job," he said. "Which it definitely was. And I saw you talking to some kids up there," he went on, moving over slightly so a woman and a toddler could go by. "Are they friends from your class?"

Now Rosie wasn't happy to see him at all. "No, they aren't nice," she said.

Dad's expression was very serious as he looked down at her. "Remember about how you need to be nice if you want other kids to be nice?" he asked. "Did you do something that might have hurt feelings?"

It sounded like Dad was the super-spy, not just Mom. "Not on purpose," Rosie said. She poked her toe in a little puddle of pool water and used it to draw a line on the concrete.

"It's important to remember that other kids have feelings too," Dad said. "And to be respectful of those feelings."

"Okay," she said. "I'm going to do a big cannonball now. You can watch me."

Dad's shoulders slumped slightly but he nodded, then headed back to where the Baileys had set up camp with their towels, water bottles, and lots of sunscreen.

Rosie marched toward the diving section, but when she noticed Charlotte sitting on the steps of the shallow end with two girls, she hurried over. "Hi," Rosie called. Charlotte would be way more fun than Dad.

"Oh, hi," Charlotte said in a voice that did not really sound like Charlotte.

"Who's this darling little girl?" one of Charlotte's friends asked. She was wearing a two-piece bathing suit that showed her stomach and only had her feet in the water. The other girl had on heart-shaped sunglasses and she was sitting next to Charlotte on the first step.

Rosie smiled.

"My sister, Rosie," Charlotte said. "Rosie, this is Sophia and Mari, my friends from school."

"Does your sister paint your nails for you?" Sophia asked. She began swishing her feet gently in the water.

"No, that's too boring," Rosie said. "But we do play d—"

Charlotte stood up so fast Rosie nearly let out her own screech of doom. "Rosie, did you do the slide yet?" Charlotte asked.

"Yeah, twice," Rosie said, not sure why Charlotte needed to interrupt, especially since Rosie had been planning to invite Charlotte's new friends over to play dolls with them.

"Oh, you guys aren't going to believe this!" Mari said with a gasp. She had lowered her sunglasses and was looking over toward the front entrance of the pool. "Cecilia Baxter is here, and check out that bathing suit."

Rosie looked over and saw a girl walking with a younger boy. She was wearing a pink bathing suit. Rosie squinted, but didn't notice anything special about it.

"It looks like the kind of suit I wore when I was five." Sophia laughed. "I mean really, who still wears pink in sixth grade?"

Mari and Charlotte giggled, but Rosie didn't think it was very funny. Or very nice. "I like pink," she informed Sophia, who smiled at her in a way Rosie didn't care for, like she knew a secret Rosie didn't.

"Of course you do, sweetie," she said. "Pink is fine when you're a little girl."

Rosie opened her mouth to tell Sophia her thoughts about that, but then she felt a hand clamp down on her shoulder. A very heavy hand. "Rosie, were you going to go to the slide? Or the diving board? I'll watch you if you want." Charlotte was giving Rosie a very serious look.

Rosie considered protesting, but Charlotte's friends were kind of boring—the diving board would be more fun after all, especially with an audience.

"Promise?" she asked.

Charlotte nodded. "Yes, definitely," she said.

So Rosie continued on toward the diving board, excited to impress the girls with her jump.

The line wasn't that long, though there were three big boys standing in front of her shoving one another and laughing.

"Watch it," Rosie said when one of them bumped into her.

The boy didn't even seem to hear her.

"Hey, isn't that Sergeant Wimpy?" the tallest one asked, pointing toward the soaker section of the pool. "Maybe we can get him to reenact that picture."

The other boys looked over and Rosie did too, but she didn't see anyone who looked like a sergeant at all. As she scanned the pool area, she did see her brother sitting next to one of the soakers. It was so big, he was almost hidden behind it. In fact, if he was playing hide-and-seek it would be a great spot for hiding.

"It's your turn, Chase," a girl called to the tall boy. He stopped laughing with his friends and headed up the ladder.

"Tom!" Rosie called, turning back to her brother. "I'm going to do a cannonball. Watch me!"

Tom didn't see her at first so she waved both hands over her head. He bit his lip and took a step back when he saw her. Clearly he was worried the diving board was too high.

"Don't worry, I can do it!" Rosie shouted.

It was finally her turn, so she grabbed the sides of the ladder and began climbing up. It really was high. Rosie paused, squinting down at the people swimming. The water was awfully far away. But Rosie was no chicken, so she took a deep breath, ran to the end of the board, and jumped.

Her heart was nearly thumping out of her chest, and she might have let out a tiny little scream, but she hit the water with a terrific splash, then sank nearly to the bottom. Rosie was utterly exhilarated as she swam up to the surface, laughing when she broke through. That had been amazing! She paddled quickly to the side and looked around. Dad was clapping from where he was sitting with a few of their neighbors, clearly impressed with her. Charlotte gave her a thumbs-up and Tom waved briefly before disappearing into the locker area.

Rosie beamed, proud of how brave she was and excited to do it again.

But as she pulled herself out of the pool she caught sight of Aisha sitting on a big shark towel with Oscar. Debbi was with them, along with Ainyr and Khai, who were also in Rosie's class. They were sharing a pack of gummy bears and laughing. Looking at them together, all cozy on the towel, gave Rosie a hollow feeling right at the center of her chest.

Just then some water hit Rosie on the back, as though someone had splashed her on purpose. Rosie turned to give this person a very indignant look, but the woman, who was not being careful as she got out of the pool, was too busy talking to her friend to take any notice of Rosie.

"She was gone all night, and she's never been gone more than an hour before," she said, sniffing a little, her soft Southern accent making the words sound even more tragic. Water ran down her braids, hung on the colored beads at the ends, and fell onto her striped blue bathing suit.

"Pepper's just having a little adventure," the other woman said, squeezing water out of her long brown hair. "Dogs like to explore, but I'm sure once she gets hungry, she'll be back."

The first woman shook her head, making the beads clink together. "No, she already missed dinner last night and breakfast this morning," she said, now sounding tearful. "I think it's safe to say that Pepper's gone missing."

Missing. The word echoed in Rosie's head as the two women headed toward the locker room. This dog, Pepper, had disappeared, just like Buddy. An iciness crept over Rosie despite the hot sun, because now what had just seemed strange was what Mom would call a pattern. Two dogs missing could be a coincidence . . . or it could mean something was going on.

And Rosie, who had promised Cupcake a reunion with Buddy, was going to get to the bottom of it.

★ CHAPTER 10 ★

Charlotte was at the register in the cafeteria playing with her salad fork as the cashier swiped her card. Sophia and Mari were already at their table, and she was eager to join them.

"Hey, Charlotte," Tash said, coming to stand in line behind her.

"Hi," Charlotte said, smiling at her neighbor and then taking her card back from the cashier.

As she had mentioned when they first met, Tash was really busy with band practice. She left for school before the Baileys, and Charlotte rarely saw her in the cafeteria. Though now that she thought about it, Charlotte realized it was also possible Tash was there and she hadn't noticed because she was so busy with Sophia and Mari.

She gathered up her tray, eager to get over to their table now. "See you later," she said, making her way toward the sunny table.

People greeted her as she passed, something she was

still getting used to but in a good way, like getting used to candy for dinner every night or unlimited allowance. She was so distracted by all the new faces that she nearly crashed into three boys who were sneaking looks at a phone.

"Hey," she said, finally setting her tray down on their table. Sophia and Mari were talking, but they both looked up and smiled at her.

"I've been getting so many compliments on my nails, thanks to you," Sophia said, striking a pose with her hand held next to her face.

"They look awesome," Charlotte said, settling in at her seat. Sophia had used the tape to make different-sized stripes in three colors on gold nails, and Charlotte wasn't surprised that people noticed. Of course, they noticed and complimented most things about Sophia, but still, her nails looked great.

"Using tape is such a good trick," Sophia said. "I never would have thought of it. You really are brilliant, Charlotte."

"Actually I didn't think of it either," Charlotte admitted. "I read it online."

"You still get to take credit for it," Sophia said firmly as she mixed up her salad so that her dressing was evenly distributed. Charlotte emptied her whole packet of dressing onto her salad—she'd discovered that was the best (and possibly the only) way to make the salads taste good.

"Okay, you guys, the question for today is, do we think Melanie Whitman was out last week because she had lice?" Sophia asked with a wicked smile.

"Ew!" Mari screeched.

"That would be so gross," Charlotte added, fizziness bubbling in her belly. These moments when Sophia smiled her wicked smile and Mari's eyes shone, the three of them sharing a delicious secret together, gave Charlotte the frothy, sweet sensation of a newly opened can of root beer.

Of course she always made sure these things did stay a secret. Like now she looked around to make sure Melanie was far away so she wouldn't hear them. Charlotte was sure that as long as no one ever knew, these little scraps of gossip were harmless—fun for her and her friends but never actually hurting anyone.

"She was absent on the second day of school, which is weird," Sophia said, tipping her head slightly to sneak a look at Melanie, who was sitting at a table in the middle of the cafeteria. When Charlotte looked over a second time she noticed that Tash was now at the table too, along with two other girls including Cecilia of the pink bathing suit.

"Yeah, and she got that short haircut over the weekend," Mari added as she speared a grape tomato from her salad. "Charlotte, last year she was always playing with her hair, trying to get everyone to notice it, so the fact that she'd just cut it all off is definitely fishy."

"Totally," Sophia agreed.

Charlotte knew firsthand that lice could be treated with special shampoo and a major house cleaning because she'd actually gotten lice in first grade. But she had no plans to mention that or the fact that the haircut might not mean anything. And anyway, it wasn't like she was an expert—the haircut *could* have been lice related.

"I'm staying away from her," Mari said, curling her lip disdainfully.

"We all should," Sophia declared. Charlotte nodded. It wasn't like any of them hung out with Melanie anyway. She'd never know the difference.

"Who should we avoid?" It was Jen Sebastian. She had a habit of stopping by their table at least once per lunch period. Not that she was the only one—a lot of girls found reasons to stand and talk to the most popular girls in the grade, and it was one of the many things that made their table so fun.

"Melanie," Mari said, tilting her head toward where Melanie was eating a sandwich, unaware of what was being said about her. "She had lice the first week of school."

Charlotte shifted slightly in her seat as Jen gasped in horror. Part of her worried that this went just a little too far, because it wasn't like they knew for sure Melanie had had lice. But on the other hand, she certainly *could* have, and it was fun to watch Jen react so dramatically. Jen would probably forget about it in five minutes anyway.

"Yuck, I am not getting near her," Jen said. She glanced at Melanie and shuddered slightly.

"Charlotte, I forgot to tell you how cute your sister is," Sophia said, turning slightly away from Jen, who took the hint and headed toward her own table. "What's her name again?"

"Rosie," Charlotte said, pleased to hear her sister complimented. Though when she remembered Rosie's near slip about the dolls, she shuddered—it would have been awful to have Sophia and Mari find out Charlotte still played like a little kid sometimes.

"She's sweet," Sophia said, uncapping her seltzer and taking a sip.

"Yeah," Charlotte said, though *sweet* might not be the first word that came to mind when she thought of her tornado of a little sister.

"You guys have to see this." It was Jen again, but this time she was not alone. Grace Chen and Tanya Santangelo were with her, both giggling as they looked at Charlotte.

"What is it?" Sophia asked, clearly intrigued.

"It's this picture Chase Hammond took," Jen said, nearly dancing with glee that she got to be the one telling Sophia the latest gossip. Though Charlotte wasn't sure why the three of them kept looking at her.

"How did you get it?" Mari asked.

"The boys were all passing it around this morning," Jen said.

Charlotte remembered the boys who almost ran into her earlier—they were looking at a phone and laughing.

"And my brother got it and sent it to me just now," Grace said.

"Isn't your brother in eighth grade?" Mari asked.

"Yeah, but he and Chase both play JV football,"

Grace explained. "And Chase sent it to everyone on the team."

"Sounds juicy," Mari said, eyes sparkling. "Show it to us."

Grace sat down next to Sophia and looked around for the cafeteria aides before sliding her phone out of her pocket and quickly setting it flat on Sophia's tray so no one looking from a distance would know it was there.

"What's it of?" Sophia asked while Grace typed in her passcode.

"Charlotte's brother, Tom," Jen said. Tanya snorted with laughter when Jen said his name, and Charlotte's back stiffened. Why was this boy Chase taking pictures of Tom? And why was Tanya looking at Charlotte like she was the punch line to a joke?

"Here it is," Grace said triumphantly.

Charlotte's throat and mouth were dry, as if she'd swallowed a handful of sand, and when she looked down at the image it was all she could do to keep breathing. *Now* she knew why Tom had been so quiet, so distracted. He must have known about this photo, the one where his mouth was open, his eyes wide in shock like a crazed cartoon character, his hands clawing the air in front of him. He looked as if he was being attacked by a grizzly bear or a pack of wolves, but anyone viewing the picture could see the truth: Tom was terrified of a little stream of water. He looked beyond ridiculous, like the biggest scaredy-cat in the world, like a boy who was about to become the laughingstock of the school.

A boy who was going to take his sister along for the ride.

★ CHAPTER 11 ★

"Hey, Sergeant Wimpy," a boy from Tom's homeroom called, snorting with laughter as Tom passed by at the end of lunch period. He twisted up his face like someone being electrocuted, mimicking Tom's expression in the now-famous photo.

Tom kept his eyes pinned on a point in the distance, doing everything he could to keep his head high and ignore the laughter that swirled around him. Which was impossible, of course. Because ever since he had arrived at school that morning, the picture was all he heard about. Boys snickered about it when he walked by, joked about it in the locker alcove next to him, and imitated it on the way to class. By the time the bell for lunch rang, everyone he passed had called him Sergeant Wimpy. And the worst part was, Tom was pretty sure they were right.

Before his family had come to Fort Patrick, Tom had never thought much about whether or not he was brave.

Sure, there was the screech of doom, but his family merely said Tom was high-strung or that he startled easily. It was only now that Chase had humiliated him in front of the entire school that a seed of doubt had been planted. A seed that had Tom rethinking everything. Why *did* he startle at tiny things? And why had he screamed so loudly over a little spray of water and then said nothing when Chase made fun of him? Was it possible that Chase had said what everyone secretly thought, that Tom was a wimp?

Kenny was putting books in his locker and lifted a hand in greeting when he saw Tom. Before Tom could react, a group of seventh-grade boys ran by. One of them stopped short and threw his hand to his head in a sharp salute. "Good afternoon, Sergeant Wimpy!" he barked, and his friends burst into loud giggles.

Cheeks burning, Tom bolted around the corner to escape, but then he stopped dead in his tracks because coming toward him was Chase. He was surrounded by his friends, all grinning as they caught sight of Tom. Chase's face glowed and he strode down the hall like a quarterback who had just scored the winning touchdown.

Tom didn't think, he simply acted, spinning around and nearly sprinting back down the hall, away from

Chase and his friends. But of course their laughter and their jeering followed him as Tom pushed his way blindly into the bathroom and locked himself in a stall.

He leaned back against the wall, closed his eyes, and tried not to think about how running to the boys' room to hide had pretty much cemented his status as a one-hundred-percent total wimp.

The day dragged on in a state of endless humiliation. Tom wondered if maybe Charlotte would find him to say something sympathetic, but she barely glanced at him in the one afternoon class they had together. Kenny gave him a sympathetic shoulder pat, but other than that, it was all Sergeant Wimpy all the time. So when detention finally ended, Tom was desperate to get away from school and back home to his family. Because even if they did secretly think he was a wimp, they were kind enough not to say so. And they never called him names.

Tom headed outside where he saw the first good thing to happen all day: Charlotte was waiting for him.

"Hey," Tom called, so happy to see her he actually smiled, something he hadn't thought he'd ever do again.

Pouring out the horrors of his day to his sister and getting full sympathy for the wounds that had been sliced open by Chase and his classmates might not make things better but it would help. Maybe Charlotte would even suggest stopping for ice cream and offer to treat.

But when Tom reached his sister, he realized that he had missed a few obvious signs that the offer of ice cream was not going to be coming any time soon. Charlotte's eyes blazed and her cheeks were a mottled shade of red. She stood stiff and tall, hands on her hips. And she was breathing so hard it was like she had just run a marathon.

"How could you?" she asked through clenched teeth. "How could you do this to me?"

Tom took a step back. "What-what do you mean?" he stuttered. "Chase attacked *me* and—"

"And you freaked out and he took a picture, I *know*," Charlotte raged. "Everyone knows! It's all anyone is talking about."

On their first beach day in Hawaii, Tom had been knocked over by a huge wave. Salt water had filled his nose and ears as his body was flipped about in the water so completely that at one point he had no idea which way was up and which was down. That was how he felt now as he tried to understand why his sister was mad at him, not at Chase or any of the kids who had mocked him all day. Charlotte was acting like he had done something horrible to hurt her when in fact he was the one who had been hurt.

"What's up, Sergeant Wimpy?" a boy who was clearly an eighth grader shouted, giving Tom a salute.

"Now even the older kids are doing it," Charlotte hissed. "You couldn't even bother to tell me, to prepare me?"

Tom blinked, unable to process why she was so angry at him. He was the one who was a laughingstock—the boy hadn't even noticed Charlotte. "I don't get it," he said. "Why are you yelling at me?"

"Because you're ruining everything," Charlotte told him, then turned and stalked down the sidewalk, away from Tom, who stared after her, his last ally now turned against him, leaving him totally alone.

CHAPTER 12

M s. Gupta, Rosie's teacher, glanced at the clock on the back wall of the classroom. "Okay everybody, that's all for today. Tomorrow we'll start working on our posters for math, so you and your partner can begin coming up with your example problems. Right now, go ahead and line up."

She smiled cheerfully, saying good-bye as the children filed out into the hall with the class aide. Normally Rosie gave her a hug good-bye. *Normally* Rosie liked Ms. Gupta, who came up with good ideas like reading aloud in fun voices and doing jumping jacks before math. But today Ms. Gupta had come up with the worst idea ever: partner work for the math poster.

Ms. Gupta had said students could choose their own partners, and everyone got very excited, waving to friends and pairing up. Everyone except Rosie, because no one wanted to be her partner. Which was fine— Rosie already had an idea for the poster and could easily do it herself. But Ms. Gupta had put Rosie together with

Victor, the quiet boy who no one wanted to work with either.

So instead of saying good-bye to Ms. Gupta and Isabelle the Iguana the way she usually did, Rosie just stomped out of the classroom. Ms. Gupta was probably sad and worried not to get to say good-bye to Rosie, but that was her very own fault for making the math poster partner work.

The aide led Rosie's class to the big metal front doors of the school where students were filing out, something that could take a while because there were a lot of students and not a lot of doors. Rosie shifted from one foot to the other, wishing everyone would get a move on so she could get outside already.

"Don't push," a girl named Taima told her.

"I'm not!" Rosie said quickly. Maybe her hand had touched Taima a little, but she was in the way.

Finally Rosie was walking down the stone steps of the school, blinking in the bright sun as students streamed past.

"Rosie!" It was Dad! This was an excellent surprise, as Rosie usually walked home herself, with the help of the crossing guards on every corner.

"I had a break in my work so I decided to come meet you," Dad said after Rosie had run up to him.

"It was a terrible day," Rosie said, eager to get Dad's sympathy.

"I have an idea on how we might turn it into a good day," Dad said, not even asking what had gone wrong.

Rosie waited, hoping the idea involved ice cream or a special adventure, just her and Dad.

"Why don't we invite one of your classmates over for a playdate?" Dad asked.

Rosie was horrified. "That's not a good idea at all," she told Dad reproachfully.

"What if we just gave it a try?" Dad said. "I bet a lot of kids would enjoy meeting Cupcake."

Well, that was probably true, because Cupcake was the best dog ever. But Rosie didn't think any of her awful classmates deserved to meet her dog.

"That girl looks nice," Dad said. He pointed at Sam, a girl who sat near Rosie and was nice about sharing markers. But just then Taima and Nghia ran over to Sam and the three of them walked off together.

"They're busy," Rosie said, hoping that would be the end of it.

"Okay, well, how about that boy?" her dad asked. "He's looking over at us, and I bet he's very nice."

Rosie spun around, and when she saw the boy her dad was talking about she shook her head so hard her braids flew, but it was too late. Dad was already waving the boy over.

"What's your name?" Dad asked, all friendly like Cupcake when a new person came to their home.

Victor blinked his red, watery hippo eyes like he was unsure how to answer that question. "Victor," he finally said so quietly Dad had to bend down to hear. "Rosie and I are doing our math poster together."

A woman in a yellow sundress suddenly popped up behind him. "Hi, I'm Carmen," she said, shaking Dad's hand. "Victor's aunt. He was hoping Rosie could come over to bake cookies today and maybe brainstorm a bit about their math poster."

"What a lovely idea," Dad said. He sounded way too happy. "Rosie would really enjoy that."

That was not true at all. The only thing Rosie would enjoy would be going home for a snack and a sulk and then searching for clues about Buddy. Now that she had learned a second dog on post had gone missing, she was sure something very fishy was happening at Fort

Patrick. Unfortunately Tom and Charlotte weren't convinced yet, but Rosie was working on it, and she needed the afternoon to investigate, not spend time with boring old Victor.

But Dad was giving her his most serious look, and Rosie knew what that meant. "Okay, I guess," she said.

Now Dad's mouth was pinching up.

"And thank you for inviting me, ma'am," Rosie added quickly.

That earned her a smile from Dad. As the four of them walked to Bingham Road together, Victor stayed quiet, scuffing his shoes as he walked, but at one point he looked at Rosie and smiled shyly. Rosie did not smile back. Sure, Victor seemed okay, but he'd probably be all bossy about the cookies, telling Rosie what to do, and then try to be in charge of their poster.

Victor's house was across the street from the Bailey home. Dad waved good-bye, and Aunt Carmen held the door open for Rosie. When she walked in, Rosie had to wrinkle her nose at the strong scent of pine cleaner. Everything was neat and tidy with no specks of dust or stray shoes or books left anywhere.

"Your house could pass inspection," Rosie said.

Aunt Carmen laughed. "We like things neat."

Victor nodded, but Rosie couldn't tell if this was what Victor really thought.

"Okay, let's get these cookies started," Carmen said, leading the way down a hall that had a tan carpet with straight vacuum lines making stripes down the middle. "Rosie, do you like chocolate chips?"

"Everyone likes chocolate chips, silly," Rosie said, then clapped a hand over her mouth.

But Aunt Carmen just laughed. She was definitely more fun than Victor, so Rosie was disappointed when she helped them get out the ingredients but then left to write some emails. Rosie poked at the bag of chocolate chips while Victor got a mixing bowl from the cabinet. Their kitchen looked almost exactly like the Baileys' kitchen, with lots of cabinets, a big counter, and a blue checkered linoleum floor. Though their floor did not have scuff marks from dog paws like Rosie's house did, nor artwork up on the walls and fridge. The Bailey kids always drew pictures for the kitchen in every new place they lived. It was a tradition. But here the walls and fridge were bare.

"I'm an excellent baker, so my aunt lets me be in charge of mixing," Victor said proudly. He was putting on a kid-sized apron printed with spatulas.

"With the electric mixer?" Rosie asked eagerly. That could be good.

Victor blinked a few times. "No, with a spoon," he said. "I can't use the electric one by myself."

Rosie sagged a bit at this news.

"Do you want to crack the eggs?" he asked.

Now things were getting interesting. Tom and Charlotte never let Rosie crack the eggs.

"Yes," Rosie said immediately, excited again.

It took six eggs for Rosie to finally get enough slithery stuff into the bowl, but Victor didn't get bossy or try to take over. He just waited until she was done. He also let Rosie measure the sugar and didn't seem to mind when she put in double.

"I like things sweet too," he said.

Rosie let him do the flour and baking soda and they both put in the chips, eating some along the way. Then they used spoons to put blobs of dough on the sparkly cookie sheet. Rosie had a hard time getting her blobs all the right size, but Victor didn't act like it was a big deal, the way Charlotte would have, when Rosie had to use her fingers to even things out.

When the tray was ready, Aunt Carmen came in and put it in the oven. "I'll keep an eye on these," she said. "You kids go start your math homework, and I'll call you when they're done."

Rosie's spirits collapsed. Yes, it had turned out Victor was okay to bake with, but now he'd probably want to make their poster boring and argue if Rosie wanted to draw fun things on the side. Rosie hoped those cookies would be ready fast as she followed Victor into the living room.

"I'll get some paper so we can write our examples down," Victor said. Their poster was going to be about the rules of adding, and Ms. Gupta had explained that each set of partners should come up with four good examples. "That way we can start coloring our poster tomorrow in class."

Victor went over to a wooden dresser that was covered with photos. Several were of a man in uniform, and Rosie figured that was Victor's dad or uncle. Victor slid open a drawer and pulled out some paper.

"Did you find what you were looking for?" he asked, coming back with paper and pencils and sitting down on the sofa next to Rosie.

Rosie's forehead crinkled. "What do you mean?"

"When I saw you last week you were looking for something," Victor said. Rosie was impressed that he had such a good memory. She had forgotten all about seeing him.

"Maybe I can help you find it," Victor said, playing with a pencil. "I'm good at finding things."

Rosie considered this. On the one hand, she didn't want his help, but on the other hand, he had lived on post longer than Rosie and her family. He might know something about the two missing dogs that would help Rosie in her investigation.

"You can't help me search," Rosie said, to be sure Victor did not get his hopes up. "But you can tell me if you know them."

"Who?" Victor asked, looking wilted at the bad news of not being able to be part of the action.

"Two dogs," Rosie said. "I call the first one Buddy. He's a German shepherd with a black nose. And then the other one is a dog named Pepper."

Victor paused and then shook his head. "I don't know anyone in our neighborhood with those dogs," he said. "But there are a lot of people I don't know."

This did not surprise Rosie.

Victor looked at Rosie hopefully. "Are you sure you don't want help? I'm a good detective; that's what my dad says."

That might be true, but he was still not invited.

"No thanks," Rosie said. She felt slightly bad when Victor's eyes got a little watery, but he could find his own thing to search for; he didn't need to glom on to hers and try to take over.

"I like dogs, especially German shepherds," he said a woebegone voice. "That's the kind of dog my dad has. His name is Sunshine and he's a Military Working Dog."

Rosie was interested despite herself. "That's cool," she said. "What kind of work does your dad do?"

"He leads a squad that defuses bombs," Victor said.

That sounded very exciting and daring to Rosie, though the name of his dog did not. "Sunshine isn't a brave name," she pointed out.

Victor nodded. "I know, but my dad said the breeders get to name the dogs, and sometimes the names are kind of funny. He said he once met a dog named Kitty."

Rosie had to laugh at that.

"He sends me pictures of Sunshine sometimes," Victor went on. He was looking at the photo on the table.

"Did he send you one today?" Rosie asked. She wanted to see Sunshine for herself.

But Victor shook his head. "I don't know if Sunshine's with my dad anymore."

"Why not?" Rosie asked, surprised. She thought MWDs always stayed with their handlers.

"My dad's in the hospital in Germany," Victor said. Rosie knew about this hospital. It was where overseas soldiers went if they were badly injured. Mom once had a friend there whose leg got very hurt in an explosion. "Dad's been there for a while, and Mom went over to stay with him."

"Will he be okay?" Rosie asked.

"No one knows yet," Victor said in a scratchy voice. "They're still waiting for him to wake up." He sniffled as he looked at the picture of his dad.

Victor's eyes were extra red and watery now. But this time he did not remind Rosie of a sick hippo.

Rosie cleared her throat. "I changed my mind," she said. "You can help me look for Buddy and Pepper after all."

Victor looked at her, blinked a few times, and then smiled a very big smile.

"There's just one thing," Rosie said quickly, before he could get the wrong idea. "*I'm* the one in charge."

★ CHAPTER 13 ★

The terrible events of the day that had culminated in Charlotte screaming at him had left Tom shell-shocked. He needed some time to recover and regroup, and to devise a new strategy to get Chase to leave him alone. So instead of heading home after Charlotte screamed at him, Tom struck out in the other direction, down Washington Street, through the central plaza and then onto Adams Drive.

The sun beat down, and Tom rubbed some sweat from his temples as he wandered past a training field, then stopped at the obstacle course. Another platoon was out running drills, but this time they were working together in small groups. Tom watched as two soldiers lifted a third up to the top of the tall wooden wall in the middle. The second soldier then got a leg up from the first, as well as a hand up from the third, and then both reached down to pull the first soldier up. Tom remembered how the last time each soldier had struggled on his or her own to reach the top. It went a lot faster this way.

But of course thinking about that made Tom remember that the last time he was here he had been with his sisters and Charlotte had still liked him. The fact that his sister was furious with him, which Tom was still puzzling over, sat heavy and sharp in his chest, like a coil of barbed wire.

Tom's face was baking, his lips were dry from the sun, and he realized he was parched. Dad always made sure they had money for emergencies tucked into their backpacks, and Tom figured dehydration counted, so he headed to Patrick Boulevard and the small deli next to the movie theater.

"Hey there, partner," the friendly man behind the counter said as Tom walked in, the chill of the air conditioner instantly soothing on his sweaty skin.

"Hi," Tom said. This was the first time in hours anyone had been kind to him, and the thought made Tom feel even more alone.

"It's a scorcher out there today," the man said. He was wearing an Army Strong cap and an army-green T-shirt.

"Yes, sir, it sure is," Tom agreed, heading to the

cooler of drinks. The lemonade was calling, but as he reached for it his hand brushed the fresh-squeezed grapefruit juice.

"I don't know how those GIs do it on a day like this," the man said, shaking his head at the thought.

Tom's hand froze at the grapefruit juice, the man's words turning over in his mind. Because he suddenly realized he knew exactly how those soldiers out on the obstacle course made it through a day like today: They did it by working together. And that had been Tom's tactical error all this time. At the first sign of trouble, Tom had gone solo in his mission instead of building up a team. Now, when things had gotten dire, he was alone and defenseless, struggling up an impossible wall on his own instead of getting a leg up from the people who had his back. The people who always had his back: his sisters.

"You having trouble deciding?" the man asked.

Tom took a deep breath. "No, sir," he said, grabbing the grapefruit juice, some apple juice, and the lemonade. "I know just what I need."

Charlotte was at the back picnic table painting her nails in brushstrokes so fierce Tom thought polish was probably splattering everywhere.

"I'm sorry," he said, pushing through the screen door. Cupcake flew toward him, a bundle of joyful yipping fur. At least one member of the family wasn't mad at him. Tom patted Cupcake but almost dropped the drinks in the process. "I got this for you," he said, rescuing the grapefruit juice before it fell and handing it to his sister.

Charlotte did not reach out to take it, so Tom set it on the table next to her polish. "I should have told you about what was going on with Chase from the start," Tom said.

This time Charlotte looked up. "Why didn't you?" she asked.

Tom sat down at the table across from her and began twisting open his lemonade. "I don't know," he said. "I guess it was just embarrassing." It did not feel good to say this, but it did feel good to have Charlotte reach over and pat his arm.

"Yeah, it really is," she said.

"Hey," Tom said, snatching his arm away as Charlotte laughed. He couldn't help joining in, though.

"Okay," Charlotte said, getting serious as she put her brush back in the polish and twisted the cap shut. "So tell me about it now."

Cupcake came and rested her head on Tom's lap, and he rubbed the fuzzy spot between her ears as he told Charlotte everything, from the pocketknife to the hose to his day of being ridiculed as Sergeant Wimpy. "I don't know, maybe Chase is right, maybe I am a big wimp," Tom said. Things were better sitting here in the cool shade of the yard with Cupcake and Charlotte and the refreshing lemonade, but the thought of Chase and being called Sergeant Wimpy for the rest of his life still had Tom pretty gloomy.

"You're not, though," Charlotte said firmly.

"What about the screech of doom?" Tom asked.

"You startle easily," Charlotte said, opening up her juice. "But the thing is, everyone's scared of something. Chase might be terrified of snakes or getting stuck in an elevator."

This was very hard to picture, but Tom got her point.

"And the goal now is to get him to stop," Charlotte went on. Because of course she saw that a mission was necessary. "What are you thinking?"

"Maybe we could figure out what scares him and then take a picture of him," Tom said, inspired by Charlotte's claims that Chase had to be frightened of something.

But Charlotte shook her head. "No, that's too hard. It's not like we can force him to go skydiving if he's afraid of heights. I think our best bet is showing everyone that yeah, maybe you got startled by the water, but you're still brave."

That sounded good, much better than skydiving. Charlotte really was the best when it came to strategy.

"I should have told you about Chase that first day," Tom said. "Then it never would have gotten this bad."

"Probably not," Charlotte said in a joking, lofty tone. But then she looked at her brother and bit her lip for a moment. "I'm sorry I yelled at you after school today."

"No big deal," Tom said. It had been, but now, with Charlotte on his team, ready to help him scale the wall, it didn't matter. Still, he was glad she had apologized.

"I'm home!" Rosie shouted, racing into the yard so abruptly Tom nearly screeched.

"Dad said you had a playdate?" Charlotte asked.

"Yup. Over at Victor's house," Rosie said. She spotted her apple juice and sat down to drink it.

"That's Rosie's new friend from school," Dad said, coming out on the porch to join them. He was smiling, and Tom wondered if this was indeed true.

"Victor's okay," Rosie said, wiping some juice off her upper lip.

Now Dad beamed. "Coming from you that's high praise," he said.

Charlotte glanced at Tom and raised her eyebrows because Dad was right—that might have been the first nice thing Rosie had ever had to say about any of her classmates.

"Next time we can have him over to our house," Dad added. He was wearing his "Kiss the Chef" apron, which meant dinner preparations were under way.

"Maybe," Rosie said. "I told him he can help me find Buddy and Pepper."

"Lucky boy," Dad said with a chuckle. "But first I was hoping the three of you could help me out. I want to make biscuits for dinner, but we're black on flour. Would you guys run to the commissary and pick some up?"

Rosie grinned at the military term for being out of something essential.

"Sure," Charlotte said as Tom nodded.

Dad gave them money and one of the family's reusable shopping bags, and the three Baileys headed back out into the hot afternoon.

"Tom needs our help," Charlotte told Rosie as they passed by a moving truck parked in front of the house on the corner. Tom suspected moving trucks were on the base most days of the week, considering how often army people moved. "He needs to show some of the boys at school he's brave."

"Actually all the boys," Tom admitted with a sigh. "And the girls too. Everyone at school calls me Sergeant Wimpy." It wasn't as humiliating to say as Tom had imagined. In fact, it felt kind of good to have it off his chest, and it helped that Rosie scowled her most ferocious scowl and balled up her fists at her sides.

"Those boys are the WORST," she said darkly.

Tom nodded. "Tell me about it. And now I have to figure out how to get them to stop."

"We need to find a way to prove to them that Tom is brave," Charlotte said, lifting her hair off the back of her neck to cool off a bit.

"So we need to lie?" Rosie asked, her eyes widening.

"Hey," Tom complained, though of course Rosie had hit on his own fear.

"You were a scaredy-cat about going into Mrs. Watkins's basement in Pennsylvania," Rosie reminded him.

Rosie really wasn't helping at all.

"Okay, but the point is, if we can show everyone that Tom's brave, they'll forget about the ways he's a scaredy-cat," Charlotte said impatiently.

This was also not helping. Tom had liked it better when Charlotte was talking about how everyone was scared of something, not calling him a scaredy-cat. That was as bad as Sergeant Wimpy.

"Maybe we need a different plan," Rosie said. "We could send the soldier ghosts from the haunted house to get the mean boys."

They'd reached the parking lot of the commissary. Soldiers and families were loading up groceries in car trunks or heading inside to stock up.

"That's it!" Charlotte crowed, turning to Tom. "The haunted house. Tash said everyone's scared to go near it. If you're the first to go inside, they'll see how brave you are."

Tom considered this. On the one hand, the house was scary and the thought of going in was pretty daunting. But of course that was the point. If Tom could do it and everyone in school knew, there'd be no way they could keep calling him Sergeant Wimpy. Plus he wouldn't be alone—he'd have his sisters with him. "That could really work," he told Charlotte.

"But how will everyone know you really went in?" Rosie asked as they walked toward the big doors of the store. "They might just think you're lying."

That was true.

"We could take pictures," Charlotte said.

"Or make a video," Tom said. It could be dramatic, with him looking stoic and determined as he headed inside. Maybe they could even add a sound track.

Charlotte grinned. "Perfect."

"That'll show those mean boys," Rosie added.

"Roger that," Tom agreed, certain that with his sisters on his team, *this* mission would be a success.

★ CHAPTER 14 ★

"Hurry!" Charlotte heard Rosie yell from the front hall that Saturday afternoon. Their parents had gone shopping for patio furniture for the backyard, leaving Charlotte and Tom in charge, and the siblings were heading to the haunted house.

"Coming," Charlotte called from the bathroom where she was applying sunscreen. She'd forgotten it the other day and her cheeks were still red and peeling, a condition she did not need to make even worse. She was not looking for more reasons to stand out at Fort Patrick Middle School: Being Sergeant Wimpy's sister all week had been more than enough.

"We're going to be late," Rosie said. She ran into the closet, grabbed some supplies, then raced out of the room.

"Coming," Charlotte said again, capping the sunscreen and heading down the stairs two at a time. "Don't worry, we won't—" She stopped suddenly when she saw her sister and burst into laughter. "Rosie, you don't need your night vision goggles. It's bright sun out there."

Rosie frowned—not an easy feat in the bulky goggles. "We might need them if it's dark in the house," she explained.

"She has a point," Tom said, coming down the stairs. "Plus they look cool."

Rosie smirked at her sister.

Charlotte held up her hands. "Fine, whatever," she said. She just hoped they wouldn't run into Sophia or Mari on their way to the house. Rosie was not looking so darling right now. And Charlotte did not need them to see anyone else in her family being weird. Because of course that's what her new friends thought about her brother: That he was a weirdo Charlotte was unlucky enough to be related to. It was an attitude that grated on Charlotte . . . but also one she hadn't corrected. Yet. She kept promising herself she'd tell her friends how close she was to her brother, but really it would be so much easier to do after they made the video that proved Tom was brave. So today they'd get the video, Monday they'd show it around, and by lunch no one would even remember brave Tom had once been Sergeant Wimpy. "Do you have your phone?" she asked Tom.

"Check," Tom said, holding up his phone. "All charged and ready."

"Good, and mine is too," Charlotte said. "So let's get going and make this video!"

"Finally," Rosie said. "And while we bike over, stay on the lookout for Buddy because he's still missing. Pepper too."

Charlotte tried not to roll her eyes. "Okay, but we're going straight there. Getting the footage of Tom going into the haunted house is top priority."

"Roger that," Rosie agreed.

Charlotte was glad Rosie got how important this was. And hopefully she would forget about the dogs once they started a real investigation.

The Baileys headed out into the sunny afternoon. It was slightly cooler than it had been earlier in the week, with a soft breeze that felt good on Charlotte's cheeks as they grabbed their bikes from the garage.

"So what do you think we'll find there?" Tom asked as they pedaled down Bingham Road.

"Maybe those soldiers that got experimented on turned into zombies," Charlotte said, knowing Tom liked zombie comics. Tom probably thought she was being extra nice because she felt bad kids were mocking him so relentlessly, and of course it was true that that infuriated Charlotte. But underneath her righteous anger was the slippery guilt that made Charlotte squirmy every time she remembered how she had yelled at her brother.

She had been upset at the secret he'd kept from her. But worse, she'd also been embarrassed by him, and if she was completely honest with herself, she still kind of was. It was a wretched feeling that she desperately wanted to be rid of. In fact, Charlotte knew it was possible that she cared even more about getting this video than Tom did. She slowed her bike to a stop at the central plaza while a platoon marched past in smart formation.

"I thought the soldiers turned into ghosts that haunt the building," Rosie said. "Not zombies." She had somehow managed to wedge her bike helmet over the goggles, and she looked like a beetle.

"It could be either," Charlotte said, watching how perfectly each soldier marched, exactly in step with the person in front of them. They made it look easy, but Charlotte's class had tried it in gym and it was actually quite hard.

"Or both," Tom added uneasily as the platoon passed and they began to ride again.

There were almost no cars on Gettysburg Drive, and Charlotte sped up, her siblings right behind, as they neared Crimson Drive. Once they turned onto the quiet street, Tom took the lead so that he could show them the nearly hidden alley. Moments later, the three of them came to a stop in front of the wooden building. It was set back from the road, with uneven patches in the lawn. Charlotte noticed ruts in the driveway that seemed fresh, but the house had an abandoned feel to it, like nothing human had been there in a long time.

"It's creepy," she said quietly to her siblings. She still wasn't sure if she believed in ghosts, but if she did, they would definitely live in a place like this.

"Let's go inside now," Rosie said in her normal voice, kicking the stand on her bike and starting toward the porch.

"Wait, not too fast," Tom said, his eyes darting nervously at the wooded area behind the house.

Charlotte understood his hesitation—the way the shadows fell over the house, making it seem like twilight even in the light of day, was unsettling. And who knew what might be lurking in the woods? But they'd come to conquer the haunted house, not just stare at it.

"Don't worry, it'll be fine," she said. "And we all know the plan, right?" She was looking at Rosie as she spoke.

"Yes," Rosie said, nodding and then readjusting her goggles when they slid a bit. "Tom goes first, and you video him pretending to be brave."

Charlotte saw Tom open his mouth to protest so she spoke up quickly. "Right, and make sure not to get too close to Tom so it looks like he's alone here."

"Roger that," Rosie said.

They stowed their bikes behind a bush and Rosie led the way to the porch.

Charlotte filmed Tom walking up the steps and trying the front door. He pulled hard, but it didn't give. Locked, not a surprise. Tom peered in the side window. Charlotte zoomed in over his shoulder, excited to see what alarming things might be inside, but the entryway was just dark and empty.

"Can we break in now?" Rosie asked.

"Um, let's look in the windows first," Charlotte said, clicking off the video. It would be better to see what was inside before bursting in, especially if they didn't want Tom screeching.

"Boring," Rosie complained, tugging to see if the window was unlocked.

Tom cleared his throat. "Remember, Mom says you never go into an enemy building blind. You have to scope out what's inside first, to avoid a surprise ambush."

"Right," Rosie said, letting go of the windowsill and nodding vigorously. "Can I be first to scope it out or does Tom go first?"

"You go," Charlotte and Tom said, nearly in unison. Obviously having fearless Rosie check things out first made sense. Charlotte decided that they'd do the video of Tom when they knew what the situation was inside, instead of filming him getting spooked by something unexpected.

Rosie ran over to the bay window at the front of the house and pressed her face, goggles and all, against the glass. "It's just desks and chairs," she announced.

Charlotte approached and looked closely, but all she saw was a room full of dusty old office furniture. No sign of ghosts anywhere. Though in all fairness, Charlotte wasn't sure what kind of signs ghosts left.

The Baileys walked carefully around the house, looking in all the windows on the first floor. Charlotte noticed Rosie tugging surreptitiously on them, but they were either locked or wedged shut from lack of use. The rooms, bathed in shadow, were mostly empty save for furniture and a few cobwebs.

"If there are ghosts or zombies, they're probably in the attic," Tom said.

"That's true," Charlotte said, tilting her head to peer up. "I wish we could look in the windows of the second floor."

"Maybe we could get Dad's ladder," Rosie suggested, her eyes lighting up.

"That wouldn't exactly be subtle," Charlotte pointed out.

Rosie's mouth pinched up.

"Remember, we want to be stealth ninjas," Tom told her.

"Does that mean it's time to break in very quietly?" Rosie asked.

Charlotte couldn't help laughing at that, though Rosie did have a point. "Yeah, I think it is," she said. Going in blind would not be ideal, of course, but so far all they had was a video of Tom walking onto a porch, and that was hardly going to help them. They needed to get inside and start exploring.

Rosie clapped in glee, but Tom held up a hand. "We

still haven't looked in the basement," he pointed out. "We should do that first."

Just then a crow flew overhead, its black feathers rustling as it swooped low and let out a mournful caw before landing on a low branch on the tree above them. Charlotte drew in a breath—there was something decidedly unsettling about the way it was staring down at them. Tom was standing very still beside her, clearly spooked, his gaze focused on the large bird.

But Rosie, who hadn't seemed to even notice the crow, bounced over to the basement window next to the front porch. Charlotte grabbed Tom's arm to follow. They had to scramble through a big, leafy bush, ducking to avoid getting hit in the face by the branches, in order to get to the small window. The dirt was moist under Charlotte's knees as she crouched down and peered in. And then she gasped.

"Are those . . . *cages*?" Tom whispered incredulously beside her.

"I think so," Charlotte whispered, shifting so she could get a better look. They *were* cages, four of them in a row, all about the size of a refrigerator. Leather straps hung from a hook on the wall behind them.

"And look there, on the table," Rosie said, her voice hushed for the first time.

On the white table near the cages was a tray of sharp, glistening syringes, a carton of locks, a case of sinister-looking hooked and jagged metal tools, and a pile of very strange plastic packages.

"Is that . . . ?" Charlotte asked, pressing her nose against the window as she tried to make it out more clearly.

"I think it's *flesh*," Tom said quietly.

Charlotte's hands were shaking, but she managed to press record on her phone and held it to the window.

"Do ghosts eat meat?" Rosie whispered. "Or zombies?"

"I don't—" Charlotte began but stopped short as she was interrupted by a sound from inside the basement, low and guttural.

Tom let out the screech of doom, Rosie shouted, and Charlotte leaped up so fast she nearly fell over backward into the bush.

The sound came again, this time more of a growl, deep and threatening.

"What *was* that?" Rosie asked in a breathless voice.

"Who cares?" Tom said, his face pale. "Let's get out of here."

Charlotte had to admit she agreed, but they couldn't flee, not when they had zero good video footage. "Just do something first," she hissed, holding up the phone to capture Tom. "Pose like you're about to open the window. And look brave."

Unfortunately Tom looked completely terrified, kind of how Charlotte was feeling. She was about to tell him to fake it so they could leave this creepy place once and for all, but then they heard another sound, this one behind them. It was footsteps coming up the path, though their view of whatever was walking toward them was blocked by the bush.

Charlotte felt Tom's fingers digging into her arm and even Rosie was silent, not that Charlotte could hear much of anything besides the footfalls coming closer and the pounding of her heart.

The steps came to a halt right at the bush. Charlotte held her breath and closed her eyes, waiting for hands or claws or something even worse to reach into the shrub and grab them. But then she heard a gravelly voice begin to speak.

"Yeah, I'm at the site," a man said, then paused for a moment. "No, no one followed me. I was careful, just like we discussed."

Charlotte leaned forward as silently as she could, giving Tom a quick look when he tried to stop her. She held her breath again, so as not to make even a single leaf on the bush flutter, and looked out. There on the path stood a man talking on a cell phone. He appeared completely unaware of the three Baileys hidden behind the bush.

"Yes, he's locked up in there now," the man went on. "I'll just make sure everything's secure before I leave and then come back tomorrow to finish up."

With that he stuffed the phone back in his pocket and headed to the front door. He pulled out a set of keys and, after several false tries, managed to let himself inside and closed the door firmly behind him.

Rosie turned to her siblings. "I don't think that man is military," she whispered.

Charlotte had noticed that too. The man was wearing jeans and an odd brown jacket that seemed to be padded. His shoulders sloped, his hair was shaggy, and Charlotte was fairly certain she'd seen stubble along his jawline. Military men and women walked tall, wore uniforms on duty, had neat haircuts, and were never, ever unshaven. So clearly this man was not a soldier. "You're right," she said.

"Never mind that," Tom whispered tensely. "The real question is how are we getting out of here?"

"We can't go now; it's time to be spies," Rosie cried just a little bit too loudly. "He unlocked the door— maybe we can sneak in behind him!"

"Is someone out there?" the man called from inside the house.

Tom was up and running, pulling Rosie with him, Charlotte right behind. They raced to their bikes and climbed on, just as they heard the front door open.

"Who's out here?" the man yelled.

But the Baileys were gone, leaving only a trail of dust in their wake as they flew back up the alley, along Crimson Drive, and down Gettysburg Drive, not stopping to breathe until they'd reached the safety of their house on Bingham Road.

★ CHAPTER 15 ★

"So, did we get any video?" Tom asked Charlotte. He was feeling a little shaky from the scare. The Baileys had biked home in record time and headed straight to Charlotte and Rosie's room to debrief, Cupcake right behind them. Charlotte and Rosie sat on the floor near the dollhouse while Tom leaned against Charlotte's bed, Cupcake cuddled next to him, as he tried to catch his breath.

"Let's see," Charlotte said, tapping her camera app and holding up the screen. The first shot was Tom trying to open the front door and was nothing impressive. The next video was black.

"What's that supposed to be?" Rosie asked. She had shed her goggles when they returned home from the house, but they'd left red rings pressed into the skin around her eyes.

"I was trying to film all that creepy stuff in the basement," Charlotte said. "But I guess it was too dark for the phone."

That was too bad. Tom was sure the basement stuffed with ghoulish things would make a good start to a video.

Charlotte clicked on the last film clip. The shaking frame showed Tom's terrified face and then his mouth opening in a screech of doom. Tom's shoulders slumped. This was the opposite of what they wanted—in fact, if this video got out, he'd be Sergeant Wimpy for life.

"That was a real soup sundae," Rosie said, the corners of her mouth pulling down.

Tom decided not to remind her that the lingo was actually soup sandwich. Both conveyed the same meaning anyway: a big mess.

"Not really," Charlotte said. She had finished deleting the terrible clips and was starting to bounce a little, the way she did when she was excited about something. "I mean, the video was a disaster but there's obviously something going on at that house, and we're the only ones who know about it. So that's actually a pretty major discovery!"

Tom rubbed Cupcake's ears as he considered Charlotte's words. The video had been a fiasco, but all the evil-looking equipment and that sinister man added up to—well, Tom wasn't sure, but clearly it was something pretty shady. And if what Tash had said about everyone avoiding the building was true, then the Baileys really were the only ones who knew about it. "Yeah, it was really suspicious," he agreed.

Rosie, who had been sagged on the floor next to Charlotte, now sat up a little straighter.

"Especially that guy's conversation," Charlotte said. "All that stuff about no one finding out what he was doing there."

"And how someone is locked up inside," Tom said, frowning as he remembered the ominous statement. "Oh, man."

"Exactly," Charlotte said. "Something bad is going on in that house, and since that guy wasn't even military, I'm not sure the army knows about it."

"Should we tell them?" Rosie asked.

Tom had been thinking the same thing, but Charlotte shook her head. "No, not till we have real evidence."

"Like the video?" Rosie asked.

"Yeah," Charlotte said, twisting one of her braids thoughtfully. "I mean, this is bigger than us just making a video to prove Chase wrong. We need to figure out what this guy is up to before something awful happens.

But if we can make a video of it, exposing the truth but also showing Tom being brave, then we handle two problems at once."

That sounded like a great plan to Tom. "So what do we think is going on in that house?" he asked, rubbing his hands together. Back when they'd been convinced that their neighbor in Pennsylvania, Mrs. Watkins, was up to something, this had been one of the most fun parts: the brainstorming segment of the mission. Of course, Mrs. Watkins hadn't turned out to be an assassin, but it was obvious something sinister was going on in the building on post, and Tom was ready to speculate on just what it might be.

There was silence as each Bailey considered the question.

"You know, it's possible that guy is doing something illegal," Tom said after a minute. "But it's also possible he's in charge of a top secret mission and looking like a civilian is his cover."

Charlotte pursed her lips, then nodded. "Yeah, that's a good point," she said. "That might actually make more sense because otherwise how could he get on post? The security is really tight."

"What if bad guys snuck him in?" Rosie asked. "Or he paid a bribe?"

That was a good point too.

"Okay, that's true," Tom said. "But if he *is* doing an undercover mission, I think he's in charge of setting up some kind of jail for really dangerous spies. Those sounds we heard could have been some of the prisoners."

"Maybe he's creating a zombie army," Rosie suggested, coming to sit down on Cupcake's other side so she could snuggle with the big dog too. "Zombies moan, right?"

"Yeah," Charlotte said. "But remember how Tash said the building was haunted by the ghosts of GIs from a failed experiment?"

A shiver snaked across Tom's skin as he nodded.

"That makes me think the building is a medical testing site, and they're starting those experiments again," Charlotte said. Her eyes lit up as she explained her theory. "Like all those syringes and weird metal tools could be used for operating and injecting serums or whatever they need to create a super-soldier."

Tom drew in a breath. "That totally fits," he said, feeling very impressed by his sister's powers of deduction. Charlotte really would make a good spy.

Charlotte's cheeks turned pink, the way they always did when something pleased her. "Thanks, but we shouldn't rule out any of the other theories yet."

"That means we can't rule out zombies either," Rosie pointed out.

"Right, we can't rule out zombies yet either," Charlotte said seriously.

"So we need to go break in and find out which one it is," Rosie announced, standing up ready to go.

"We don't have time now," Charlotte said with a sigh. "Dad's going to be home soon and he needs us to help get dinner ready."

"Okay, well, then we should go tomorrow," Rosie said, sitting back down a bit deflated.

"That guy said he would be at the building tomorrow, though," Tom pointed out. "I don't think we can break in while he's there."

"That's because you're a scaredy-cat," Rosie said, and Tom glared at her.

"No, Tom's right," Charlotte said, coming to his rescue. "It's going to be hard enough to sneak in when the place is empty—we don't want to worry about making noise and having him discover us."

Tom tried not to shudder at the thought—he didn't need anyone calling him a scaredy-cat again.

But Rosie was nodding. "Yeah, if we have to throw a rock through the window it'll be really loud," she said.

Charlotte laughed. "Let's hope it doesn't come to that," she said.

Tom heartily agreed with that—destroying army property seemed like an especially bad idea.

"Can we go on Monday after school?" Rosie asked.

Tom shook his head. "I wish we could but I get out late because of detention and then there's homework."

Rosie scowled.

"We'll just have to wait and try to get inside the house next weekend," Charlotte said, sounding deflated.

Cupcake jumped up suddenly, nearly causing Tom to shriek, and ran toward the stairs. A moment later the front door opened.

"Hey, everybody," Dad called, and Tom heard Cupcake greeting him. Cupcake was a good spy too, the way she heard someone coming before human ears could pick up the sound.

"Hi, Dad," Rosie called. "Guess what we—"

Charlotte waved her hands in panic and Rosie

snapped her mouth shut, then covered it, her eyes wide. But luckily Dad seemed to have gotten distracted by Cupcake, who was frisking and jumping about, her way of asking to be fed.

"We need to keep our mission a secret," Tom reminded Rosie in a whisper. "We'll tell Mom and Dad once we find out what's going on."

"Otherwise they'll just tell us to stay away and not to ask questions," Charlotte said softly.

Rosie nodded. "Okay, sorry," she said.

"Who wants to eat dinner at the Officers' Club?" Dad said, poking his head into the room a moment later.

"Me!" Rosie shouted.

"That sounds great," Charlotte agreed.

"Yeah, I'm starving," Tom said, suddenly aware of how empty his belly felt. "And it will be cool to see the Officers' Club." Although they hadn't lived on post before, they had heard about Officers' Clubs, so Tom knew the food would be tasty and the place would be fancy.

"Great," Dad said, then clapped his hands together. "Let's put on some finery and head over to the club. Mom had to stop in at her office, so she'll meet us there."

Thoughts of dinner replaced thoughts of the mysterious activity in the building as Tom went to his room where he put on a button-down shirt and clean khaki pants. Then he went downstairs where Dad was wearing his own button-down, a tie, and khakis, Charlotte was wearing a blue dress, and Rosie had put on a pink skirt and matching pink blouse.

"We're looking good, if I do say so myself," Dad said, running a hand over his head. He'd gotten a crew cut in honor of their arrival on post, but still had the habit of reaching up to smooth his hair back.

"Let's pop fire," Rosie said happily.

Tom couldn't help laughing at that. "It's pop smoke," he corrected.

"That doesn't make sense," Rosie said as they walked outside into the balmy warmth of the late afternoon. "How is popping smoke like leaving?"

Tom actually thought this was a good point—"pop smoke" was one of those military terms that had never made much sense to him. "You got me," he said.

Dad gently tousled Rosie's hair. "My military speak isn't on par with Mom's, but I think pop smoke is used when you're getting out of a tricky situation," he said.

"You toss up a smoke grenade to distract the enemy and then slip away while their backs are turned."

"Cool," Rosie said, and Tom nodded, happy to have that one explained.

They all climbed into the minivan and settled in for the drive to the Officers' Club, which was by the golf course at the far end of the base. Tom gazed out the window as they left their cozy neighborhood, stopping at the main plaza and then turning right onto Gettysburg Drive. The left side of the wide street was army buildings: the large garage used for vehicle repair, a storage building, and then the POL, where petrol, oil, and lubricants were stored and handled. Tom wondered if there was anything secret going on there too. That was the cool thing about the post—the endless possibility of undercover missions and hidden activities. And that was on top of the awesome not-secret stuff, like the obstacle course and the pool.

Now the van was driving through a wooded area, sunlight and shadows dappling the road in front of them. When they emerged from the trees, Tom could see the shimmery blue of Lincoln Lake. There was a dock on the far side, with a boathouse next door where the family planned to go canoeing one weekend.

The Officers' Club was on the other side of the lake, overlooking the immense rolling green lawn of the golf course. Dad pulled the van into a parking spot and turned off the engine.

"It looks like a castle," Charlotte said, gazing at the club.

Tom might have called it more of a fortress, but he could see what his sister was saying. The large stone building with little turrets and a wide path lined with rosebushes leading up to it did seem like it was out of a fairy tale.

"There's Mom!" Rosie shouted.

Sure enough, Mom was standing in front of the big wooden doors of the club looking crisp and official in her dress blues. Tom's heart swelled with pride as two lower ranked officers went past and gave Mom salutes. Mom's arm whipped up, her hand held at a sharp angle as she saluted back.

After checking for cars, Dad let Rosie gallop up to Mom, who went from serious army officer to goofy Mom in half a second. She scooped Rosie up and gave her loud, sloppy kisses. "How's my girl?" Then she grinned at Charlotte and Tom. "And how're my big girl and my boy? Did you have a good day?"

Tom saw Charlotte give Rosie a pointed look.

"We just biked around and stuff," Tom said, deciding that didn't count as a lie since they really had biked and done "stuff."

"Sounds fun," Mom said, leading the way into the elegant main room of the club.

The AC felt good to Tom as he made his way across the thick carpet in his stiff leather shoes, taking in their surroundings. Tables draped in crisp white cloths were set around the room, and a buffet with silver chafing dishes and servers stood at the ready to dish up food that smelled delicious. There were fancy paintings on the wall—the ones Tom could see were of famous battles or portraits of war heroes—and not one, not two, but three huge chandeliers hung from the ceiling, dripping crystals that sparkled in the soft light.

"Mom, this is like Belle's castle," Rosie said in a hushed voice.

Mom grinned as Charlotte nodded seriously. Tom braced himself for a conversation about princesses, castles, and some new game for their dolls, but then Mom stopped and stood up extra straight.

"Colonel Sanchez, I'd like you to meet my family," she said to an older man, also in his dress blues.

"What grade are you all in?" the colonel asked, shaking each of the Baileys' hands. He had thinning hair and twinkly eyes, but the way he looked intently at the children as he spoke, as well as his straight posture, made it easy for Tom to imagine him commanding troops.

"I'm in first grade, sir," Rosie announced. "We have an iguana in our classroom and one day I'm going to get to feed her."

"That is splendid," the colonel said. "I'm confident you will do an excellent job."

For that he received Rosie's most glowing smile.

"Charlotte and I are in sixth grade, sir," Tom told the colonel.

The colonel smiled. "I'm sure you'll both work hard and do your mom proud," he said.

"Yes, sir," Charlotte agreed, while Tom gulped a little, not wanting to think about Chase and school—that would just ruin his appetite.

Colonel Sanchez said his good-byes, and the Baileys were seated at a round table not far from the buffet. The centerpiece was an artful sculpture of fresh flowers and a long, fluted candle, and each place was set with shiny silver and a big goblet.

"Why don't you three go ahead to the buffet?" Mom suggested. "I want to introduce Dad to a few more people."

Tom and his sisters made their way to the food, being sure to start at the beginning of the line and to take some salad, knowing Dad would just send them back if they tried to skip it.

"Mmm, I want these," Rosie said as they peered into a steaming chafing dish filled with fluffy crab cakes soaking in butter.

"Me too," Tom said.

Charlotte, the one Bailey who did not care for seafood in any form, opted for a fancy slice of cheese wrapped in bacon instead.

A few minutes later they had settled back at the table, their plates heaped with fried chicken, mashed potatoes, and green beans, as well as their salad and appetizers. Mom and Dad sat down with their plates a minute later and everyone dug in.

"This is yummy," Rosie said.

"Roger that," Charlotte said, around a mouthful of food.

In the brief moment of quiet while everyone enjoyed their first bites, Tom's thoughts went back to the house and his theory about the jail for escaped spies. And as he bit into his second piece of crisp chicken, he realized there was someone at the table who might be able to help, as long as he was subtle about it. So Tom finished chewing, then cleared his throat. "Mom, do posts ever have prisons, like maybe off in the woods?"

Mom grinned. "You mean Charlie's chicken farm?" she asked.

"What's that?" Rosie asked, so excited at a new military term she nearly tipped over her water glass.

"Easy there, soldier," Dad said, rescuing the glass.

"Charlie's chicken farm is what they call the prisons on post," Mom said, neatly slicing a piece of her steak. "They're for minor offenses."

"Is there a Charlie's chicken farm on our post?" Rosie asked, clearly delighted with the new term.

"Affirmative," Mom said. "It's on Tipton Drive, right next to the Military Police office."

So chances were, the building wasn't a prison, not if they already had one on post.

Tom's plate was empty and he was ready for seconds. A busboy whisked the dirty plate away, and Tom headed over to the buffet, trying to decide if he wanted to try the steak or the salmon this time around.

Once he was in front of the serving dishes he realized it was silly to choose when he could get both. He was just accepting the salmon from the server when he heard voices behind him.

"You looked like a girl out there," a man was saying, his voice oozing scorn.

Tom felt his back stiffen at the insult. In his family, "like a girl" was one of the best compliments out there and he hated to hear it used as a put-down.

He turned to see who had said it and then gulped a little. The man had a colonel insignia on his shoulder lapel, though one sleeve of his dress uniform was pinned back: He'd lost an arm, most likely in the line of duty. But that wasn't what made Tom take a small step back and scrunch down. He did that because of the boy whose shoulders were slumped as he scuffed a foot along the rug, the corners of his mouth turned down as his dad criticized him. Because that boy was Chase Hammond.

"I don't know why your mom and I bother to drive you off post for those practices," Chase's dad continued in the same scathing tone, "if you're going to drop the ball on the biggest play of the game."

Tom had heard enough, and he did not want Chase to know it. The only thing worse than being scolded in public was knowing that a kid in your class had heard. Especially when that kid was the boy you'd already named Sergeant Wimpy.

Tom picked up his plate, whispered his thanks to the server, and began slinking back to his table. But just as he passed the appetizers, his stiff leather shoe somehow caught in the thick rug, sending Tom flying and his food tumbling to the ground.

A waiter hustled over to help Tom up and clean the offending food off the floor. But there was still collateral damage from Tom's clumsiness. As the waiter pulled him back onto his feet, Tom snuck a look over toward the buffet table: Chase had seen him.

Tom looked away as fast as he could, and scurried back toward his family, though not before he had seen the humiliation and fury in Chase's eyes at having his father's words clearly overheard.

And judging by the intensity of that glare, Tom knew there was no way Chase was backing off his attacks now.

CHAPTER 16

"Bye, Isabelle," Rosie said on Thursday afternoon, waving to the stoic iguana in her classroom forest habitat.

"See you tomorrow, Rosie," Ms. Gupta said, smiling as the students filed out into the hall.

Rosie waved to her teacher as she walked out, Victor trailing behind. Ever since the day at Victor's house, Rosie had been spending time with him at school. Mostly it was okay, maybe even good. Victor often had excellent ideas, like trying to dig an underground tunnel on the playground and being super-spy ninjas in gym. But he didn't always want to play the things Rosie chose, like ball tag or swinging as high as possible on the swing set. Dad said Rosie should remember Victor had his own thoughts and feelings, and to respect them, but Rosie secretly thought Victor would be more fun if he just did what she wanted.

"I have a new lead to help you find Buddy," Victor said.

This was good news because no one else cared about finding Buddy.

"What is it?" Rosie asked, only the tiniest bit wary that he might be trying to take over.

Victor opened his mouth to respond, but then stumbled forward, almost falling, as a fifth grader rushed past and accidently slammed Victor with her backpack.

"Watch it," Rosie said sharply. She grabbed Victor to steady him. She might have some doubts about Victor, but she certainly wasn't going to allow anyone to run him over in the hall.

Despite the loud chatter and laughter in the crowded hallway, Rosie's voice carried and the fifth grader glanced back. "Sorry," she said.

"Are you okay?" Rosie asked Victor, now that she'd straightened that out.

Victor nodded but glanced nervously behind him a few times as they walked out of school. That was the thing about Victor: He was what Dad would call a worrier. That meant he was always thinking about the bad things that could happen. Rosie usually thought being a worrier was very silly: Why bother about bad things that probably wouldn't happen anyway? But now, as she watched Victor's wary expression, she wondered if maybe Victor worried because his dad was hurt and far away in the German hospital. Maybe if a bad thing like that happened, it made you feel like other bad things could happen too. And that made Rosie think that if any other fifth graders knocked into Victor, she would knock them right back, hard.

"So what's the lead you found out?" she asked as they reached the first corner and waited for the crossing guard to give them the all clear to cross the street. Dad had put her hair in braids that morning, and she twisted one of them around her finger. "About Buddy."

"Yesterday we got some good news," Victor began. "My dad is awake. He's still very sick and has trouble with remembering, but my Aunt Carmen said this is a big step."

"That's great news!" Rosie agreed, delighted. She wasn't sure what it had to do with Buddy, but she was very happy for her friend.

Victor nodded, his eyes shining. "Yes, and Aunt Carmen decided we needed to send him a package with his favorite chocolate bar. She said chocolate can help people remember."

Rosie had not heard this before, but it made a lot of sense because something as tasty as chocolate could probably help just about anything.

"And when we went to the post office to mail it," Victor continued, "we saw a sign about a missing dog." He beamed, clearly proud of his detective work.

"Was it Buddy?" Rosie asked eagerly. "Or Pepper?"

"Pepper," Victor said solemnly. "The sign said she's a cocker spaniel puppy."

Rosie sucked in a sharp breath. This meant Pepper, like Buddy, had now been missing for days.

"Pepper's owner lives around the corner from us," Victor continued. He was riffling around in his shorts pocket as he spoke. "Her name is Ms. James, and I wrote it all down in case you want to go talk to her." He produced a crumpled piece of paper and handed it to Rosie.

"This is a great lead," Rosie told him, taking the paper with the name and address printed in careful block letters. "I'm going to talk to her right now." This was the evidence she needed to convince Charlotte and Tom that dogs really *were* disappearing on post.

"I can go with you," Victor said, shuffling his feet, which Rosie knew meant he was excited. "I just have to tell Aunt Carmen."

"Okay, I'll go tell my dad, and then we can meet in front of my house," Rosie decided. There was no harm in letting Victor come along, especially since he had discovered the lead.

Victor walked up the front path of his house, wet from an earlier rain, while Rosie ran and threw open her front door. "I'm home," she announced.

Cupcake raced over and bounded in joyful circles around Rosie, who gave her a big hug. "I'll play with you later," she promised the energetic dog. "But I have an important spy mission first."

"What's that, Rosie Posie?" Dad asked, walking into the front hall.

"I'm letting Victor help me search for Buddy and Pepper," Rosie said, deciding that was enough information for Dad.

"Wonderful, an afternoon with your new friend," Dad said in a loud, goofy voice. "Have a great time."

Cupcake looked up with her begging face, clearly not willing to be left behind. And then Rosie had a terrible thought. What if *her* dog went missing? It was too awful to even imagine. "Dad, you'll watch Cupcake while I'm gone, right?" she asked.

Dad nodded. "Absolutely," he said. "You just have fun with your friend, and I'll take care of Cupcake."

"Okay," Rosie said, still slightly anxious about the safety of her beloved dog.

"Don't worry, Rosie Posie," Dad said, noticing her hesitate and clearly excited for her to go play with Victor. "Cupcake likes to sleep under my desk while I'm working. She'll be fine hanging out there till you get back."

Knowing Cupcake would be in the room with Dad, and possibly even sitting on Dad's feet, which the big dog always enjoyed, was reassuring.

"Okay," Rosie agreed, and headed out to meet Victor.

As Victor had promised, Ms. James lived just around the corner and well within Rosie's boundaries for walking by herself on the base. The yard had the same kind of dog fencing the Baileys had, and as they walked up the path to the front porch, Rosie noticed several holes had been dug around its perimeter. Clearly Pepper liked to dig, and Rosie felt a wave of distress that poor Pepper was now gone.

Rosie rang the bell, and a moment later a woman opened the door. Rosie recognized her immediately from the day at the pool, although this afternoon she wore yoga pants and an old gray T-shirt instead of the blue striped bathing suit.

"Hi, ma'am, I'm Rosie and this is Victor," Rosie said, remembering that Mom said introducing yourself was good manners. "We saw the sign about your puppy, Pepper, and we're really sorry she's missing, and we wanted to ask you some questions about it."

Ms. James paused for a moment, as though this was the last thing she had expected when she opened the door. But then she nodded and walked out on the porch with Rosie and Victor. "Well, it's nice to meet you both," she said, sitting down on the top step. "And I appreciate your sympathy—my husband and I are very worried about Pepper."

"Can you tell us what happened?" Rosie asked as she and Victor sat down next to Ms. James. A car drove by slowly and the driver waved at Ms. James, who waved back.

"Well, she was in the yard," Ms. James said. "I looked out the window right before she went missing, actually, because I heard a strange noise. A man was walking by dragging something that rattled. I didn't see what it was because the fence blocked my view, but I remember seeing Pepper digging a hole, that one right there, by the gate. And then when I called her about thirty minutes later, she was gone."

"Was the gate open?" Rosie asked, putting on her detective cap to try and find some clues. She was hoping the information might help them find Buddy too.

Ms. James shook her head. "Good thought, but no. That was the first thing I checked," she said. "And I also checked for loose boards in the fence, but they were all secure. I really don't think she could have escaped on her own."

The way she said it made Rosie shudder. "So you think someone let her out on purpose?" And then something truly terrible occurred to Rosie. "Do you think that man dognapped Pepper?" she asked in horror.

Ms. James shook her head. "I'm sure that's not what happened," she said.

But Ms. James had a look that Rosie recognized—it was a look Mom got when she talked about certain missions in Afghanistan or the time Rosie asked Dad what it meant when their friend Randi went MIA on a mission in the Middle East. It was the look grown-ups got when they didn't want to tell you something scary. And Rosie knew the scary thing Ms. James didn't want to say: that a man had stolen Pepper right from her own front yard.

Rosie's mind was racing because if Pepper was dog-napped by this man, that meant Buddy probably was too. And so the question now was, who would do such a terrible, awful thing?

"What did that man look like?" Rosie asked, trying to sound casual like a good spy. "The one who definitely did not dognap Pepper."

"Oh, I don't know," Ms. James said unhelpfully.

Victor had picked up on Rosie's urgency. "Was the man a civilian?" he asked.

That word was an electric zap that made Rosie's heart start pounding extra hard and her whole body tingle. Because Rosie was now picturing a very specific civilian, the civilian she and her siblings had seen at the creepy house off Crimson Drive.

"Yes," Ms. James said, pressing a finger to her chin for a moment. "Now that I think of it, I noticed he was wearing a brown coat, and it struck me as odd on such a hot afternoon."

The electricity crackled through Rosie like a live wire as all the pieces came together at once: the cages, the meat, the secrecy.

That terrible man was dognapping pets, locking them in cages in the basement of the isolated house, feeding them that meat, and then—well, who knew what his evil plan was? But now that she was onto him, Rosie wasn't stopping till she found out.

"We have to go," she told Ms. James as she sprang to her feet and raced down the path. The rain had started up again but Rosie didn't care.

She simply couldn't wait one more minute to tell Charlotte and Tom that she, the youngest Bailey of all, had uncovered the truth about the sinister man and the house off Crimson Drive.

CHAPTER 17

"Oh, I love that design," Sophia exclaimed. She grabbed Charlotte's hand so she could check out her nails close up.

"Thanks," Charlotte said, trying to smile. It had been a long week and it was only Thursday.

"You used tape?" Mari asked as she leaned over and admired the bronze, sage, and hot-pink geometric shapes on Charlotte's nails.

"Yes," Charlotte said. It was raining outside and the drops splattered against the big windows next to them. The gray of the day mirrored Charlotte's mood, and she wished she were home curled up with a book instead of under the harsh lights of the crowded cafeteria.

Sophia grinned. "We're learning your secrets."

"Well, not completely," Mari said, wrinkling her nose. She held out nails that looked as though they'd met with a mud puddle. "I tried to do a splattered look, but the colors mixed and it just looks dirty."

"I think you have to let each coat dry in between," Charlotte advised. She poked her fork into her salad and pushed it around. It seemed especially unappetizing today.

"Oh, that makes sense," Mari said. "I actually texted to ask you about it last night, but you never got back to me. What were you doing?"

Now both girls looked at Charlotte, who gulped a little. She and Rosie had been playing with dolls and having so much fun Charlotte hadn't even thought to check her phone. But she certainly couldn't tell Mari and Sophia that. "Um, my phone died, sorry," she mumbled.

"Hi," Jen Sebastian said. Charlotte had been so busy fending off Mari's question that she hadn't seen Jen approach, and hadn't had time to prepare for what had turned into a daily assault. And as usual, Jen did not waste any time seeking gossip. "Charlotte, how's your brother?"

"Fine, thanks," Charlotte said, taking a big bite of salad so she'd have an excuse not to talk.

"Well, he'd better not get too comfortable," Jen said knowingly. "Because I heard Chase saying that he was going to spook him with one of the worms we're dissecting in science next week."

Charlotte crunched down hard on the tasteless lettuce, hating everything about what Jen was saying. If it was true, it was mean and awful. If it was just a rumor, it was still mean and awful. And Charlotte was really tired of mean, awful things happening to her brother. And then getting tossed into her life at lunchtime.

"He shouldn't be such an easy target," Sophia said, shaking her head dismissively.

Charlotte thought of what she could say to defend Tom and set everyone straight once and for all. But the thought of Sophia's reaction made Charlotte's voice disappear somewhere deep inside her chest. She told herself that the only way to really defend Tom was to get the video and *prove* his bravery. But even knowing this did not make the queasy feeling go away.

"He's probably hoping Chase's family will get stationed at another post," Mari said, picking up her seltzer.

"I'm not sure that would even matter." Jen shrugged. "Everyone calls him Sergeant Wimpy now."

Charlotte wished Jen's family would get stationed at another post.

"He's kind of asking for it if he gets scared by a little thing like a worm in science," Sophia said.

Charlotte gritted her teeth at this. Nothing had even happened yet, but here Sophia was, acting like Tom had already totally freaked out.

"Hey, what's up, Sister Wimpy?" a boy called as he went past.

Jen burst into giggles, and Charlotte sank down in her seat. It was getting worse, not better, as the days passed. The only thing that could help now was making that video. As the girls started in on Tom again, Charlotte promised herself they'd make it happen this weekend no matter what.

That afternoon Charlotte decided to stop by the library after school and sent a quick text to Dad to let him know. She figured picking up a few new books would be a good distraction, and once she was there she ended up sitting on a beanbag in the corner rereading the first Harry Potter book, which was still her favorite. It was after five by the time she finally checked out a pile of books, stuffed them in her backpack, and headed outside.

It was drizzling and foggy, so Charlotte pulled out her umbrella as she walked down the slick steps. She had outgrown her rain boots over the summer and could already feel the toes of her sneakers getting damp as she started down the path. Umbrellas were good for keeping the top half of her dry, but she was pretty sure the bottoms of her jeans and her shoes would be wet by the time she got home.

No one else was outside on such a nasty day. As Charlotte walked down the empty sidewalk and passed the deserted playground, she slowly returned from the pleasant comfort of her book back to the real world. Her thoughts turned to the conversation over lunch. There was just no getting away from the whole Sergeant Wimpy thing and—

Charlotte drew in a sharp breath, because coming toward her was a man, his steps haphazard and unmilitary-like, his shoulders stooped. He was partly hidden in the fog, but Charlotte could see that he was wearing an odd brown leather jacket, just like the man they'd seen at the house off Crimson Drive. Was it him?

Charlotte slowed and glanced around. On one side of her was an athletic field, on the other the post rec center, locked and closed for the night. The road was deserted, with no one in sight. No one but the man, who was coming closer and closer.

Charlotte's heart thumped heavily against her ribs, and she debated turning and sprinting for home. But then she gathered herself. This was an opportunity to uncover clues about what was going on in the building, even if it was a bit on the spooky side. Anything she noticed about the man could help them with their investigation, so Charlotte stood tall, in proper army style, straightened her umbrella, and strode toward him.

The man looked to be in his late forties, with a weathered face and shaggy salt-and-pepper hair that grew longer than military regulation. He was still unshaven and the coat was thick, much thicker than Charlotte had realized the day before, and it was made from canvas, not leather. But all of those details took a backseat when she finally got within a few feet of him. She'd been so busy looking at his face and coat that she hadn't noticed the most significant thing: the object he was holding in his hand. It was long, like a baseball bat, made of solid wood, with a loop of what looked like wire on one end. Charlotte wasn't sure what it was exactly, but it was obvious it could do real damage. Just the sight of it gave her goose bumps.

The man barely glanced at Charlotte as he passed. She kept her eyes forward, taking deep breaths until he'd turned the corner. Then Charlotte ran home as fast as she could go.

"So what do you think it was for?" Tom asked in a hushed voice.

It was cozy back home in her bedroom, but Charlotte still felt shivery telling Tom and Rosie what she had just seen.

"I know! I know what it was for!" Rosie nearly shouted. "Today Victor and I did some detective work and we figured out that the man at that house is dog-napping dogs. Buddy was his first victim but now he has Pepper too."

Charlotte momentarily forgot her frightening encounter as she glanced at Tom, unsure how to let Rosie know that her theory did not make sense. From the way Tom's forehead was crinkled Charlotte could tell he was thinking the same thing.

"Um, I'm not sure that's what's going on," Charlotte said as gently as she could.

Rosie scowled. "Yes, it is," she said.

"Well, but *why* would he steal the dogs?" Tom asked.

Rosie paused—clearly she didn't have an answer for this.

"And why would he need weapons and syringes?" Charlotte added. "If he was taking dogs, he could probably just lure them with toys or dog treats."

Rosie was stumped by this too and Charlotte hoped that meant she'd let this new and totally unrealistic theory go.

"What do you think that was, the thing the man was carrying when you passed him?" Tom asked Charlotte, getting back to the matter at hand.

Just the memory of it made Charlotte's heart beat a little faster. "Maybe it was some kind of weapon to subdue the super-soldier," she guessed.

Tom nodded thoughtfully. "That makes sense," he said. "Because if someone has extra powers, it could be hard to control them, especially if the experiment goes wrong and they turn out like the Hulk or something."

"Good point," Charlotte agreed. She didn't read comics, but everyone knew the Hulk was a pretty scary guy and not someone you'd want running around the base.

"It's not for the super-soldier," Rosie said crossly. She was leaning against her bed, Cupcake at her side, and her eyes flashed as she looked at her brother and sister. "I told you, that man is a dognapper, and he's trying to get more dogs. That weapon is in case anyone catches him trying to take their dog." Now her hand rested protectively on Cupcake, who took this as an invitation for a belly rub and turned over, ready to enjoy a good scratch. "And I bet he's going to hold those dogs for ransom or sell them for thousands of dollars."

Charlotte looked at Tom and bit her lip. Obviously, Rosie was not going to let this go—instead she was going to come up with even more outlandish theories to prove she was right.

"Holding pets for ransom is not exactly a money-maker," Charlotte said again, trying to sound patient.

"And selling regular dogs isn't either," Tom added.

Rosie pressed her lips together and glared at them. "Then he's doing something else with those poor dogs," she snapped. "And we need to save them."

Charlotte let out an impatient breath. "Right now we need to try to save Tom," she said. "Next week Chase is going to scare him with a worm and—"

"Wait, what?" Tom asked, his voice squeaky as he sat up straight. "A worm?"

Charlotte was dismayed to see how panicked her brother appeared. "Yeah, I heard about it at lunch," she said. "Chase is going to spook you with one of the worms we dissect in science next week."

Tom's face was getting pale. "What if he surprises me and I do the screech of doom at school?" he whispered.

Charlotte's breath caught in her throat. That terrible possibility had not occurred to her. But if anyone at Fort Patrick Middle School were to witness that screech, well, these past weeks would be nothing compared to what Tom would endure. Tom and Charlotte both.

"We have to get that video this weekend," Charlotte said firmly. "Or else."

She could not finish the sentence, but when she saw the serious expressions on her siblings' faces, she knew she didn't need to.

They all knew what was at stake if they failed now.

CHAPTER 18

"I want mint chocolate chip," Rosie said on Friday afternoon as she stared into the big cooler at the colorful array of ice cream flavors on offer. "Or maybe cookie dough. Or strawberry fudge." It turned out the Fort Patrick ice cream shop was one of the best Rosie had ever seen and it was very hard to choose.

"Whatever you want, Rosie Posie," Dad said agreeably. He was licking his cone of salted caramel and did not seem in a rush to get to the PX, their next stop before returning home for dinner.

Her siblings were waiting right outside the store. Charlotte had gotten her usual Heath Bar Crunch, and Tom had ordered boring plain chocolate, though Rosie noticed he wasn't actually eating it. His cheeks were pale, and he barely glanced at Cupcake bouncing happily between him and Charlotte, hoping for a bite of the cone.

Dad had not wanted to bring Cupcake on the outing, but of course Rosie had insisted. With a dognapper loose, the base was not a safe place for Cupcake, and Rosie had no intention of leaving her unguarded, not for one second. Well, except when she had to go to school, but Dad had been looking after Cupcake then.

"I think I'll have confetti," Rosie finally decided. The most colorful ice cream was probably going to be the best.

The woman behind the counter nodded, then plopped a big scoop of the pink, blue, yellow, and purple ice cream on top of a sugar cone and handed it to Rosie. Rosie took a big lick and was rewarded with a sugary-sweet explosion.

"Good?" Dad asked as he handed over money.

"Affirmative," Rosie said, then licked around the edge of the cone to prevent drips.

Dad led the way out into the steamy afternoon. Rosie loved the feel of the hot sun on her face while she licked the deliciously cold ice cream.

The Baileys headed for the PX, walking slowly past the movie theater, where people were starting to line up for the late-afternoon show.

"Hi, guys."

Rosie turned and saw Tash had come up.

"Are you going to see the movie?" Charlotte asked.

Tash nodded. "My mom is really into movies, so we come almost every week," she said. "Have you guys been yet?"

Couples and families ambled past, some heading to the ice cream parlor, which now had a line out the door, and others toward the pizza place across the street.

"Not yet," Charlotte said. "We've been kind of busy. But hopefully soon." Her words were nice, but Rosie could tell that her sister was worried by the way she was biting at her lip instead of eating her ice cream. Even worse was Tom, who had just dumped his uneaten cone in the trash when Dad wasn't looking.

Tash nodded. "Before they start previews, everyone stands up for 'The Star-Spangled Banner,' like at a ball game."

"Do you put your hand on your heart like for 'Retreat'?" Rosie asked.

Tash nodded and smiled in a friendly way Rosie liked. "Sure do," she said.

"Maybe sometime you can come over to our house," Rosie said, certain that this would help cheer up Charlotte, at least a little. "We have a really good dollhouse."

Charlotte gave a strangled cough as Tash's eyes lit up. "I love dolls," she said.

"You can come anytime," Rosie said. "Except not now, because we're going to the PX. And not this weekend, because we have an important secret mission. But after that."

The corners of Tash's eyes crinkled as she smiled. "Okay, maybe after that," she said, then headed back to her mom.

"Let's go, troops," Dad called. He had finished his cone and now seemed eager to tackle their next errand of getting new rain boots for everyone.

As they headed down Patrick Boulevard, Cupcake danced at Rosie's heels, looking up longingly at her ice cream.

"Remember, sugar isn't good for her," Dad said. He knew it was hard for Rosie to resist when Cupcake begged.

When they arrived at the PX, Rosie realized they could not take Cupcake into the store. But luckily there were some neighbors, including Ms. Dunbar, holding a small bake sale out front, and they agreed to keep an eye on Cupcake while the Baileys shopped.

"Make sure you don't take your eyes off her," Rosie instructed.

Ms. Dunbar nodded seriously. "Don't worry, I won't," she promised. Then she glanced at Dad. "Good luck in there—it takes a brave person to try and shop at the PX on payday."

Dad rubbed his head for a moment. "Oh, I'd forgotten it was payday," he said.

Rosie didn't understand why Dad looked so worried, but once they'd walked through the doors of the huge box store she got it—it turned out that payday made everyone on post run to the PX as fast as possible. The aisles were jammed with people and carts, kids were running wild, and register lines seemed to stretch on forever. After giving up on getting a cart through the crowd, Dad sent Charlotte and Tom to get their boots farther down the aisle while he helped Rosie. But unfortunately the only pair in her size was not right.

"I don't like the blue boots," Rosie told Dad. "I definitely want pink."

"But, sweetie, these are the only ones that will fit you," Dad said, pressing his forehead the way he did when he had a headache. All the voices around them were kind of loud.

Rosie was about to tell him to take an aspirin, which was what Mom said to do when he had a headache, but then someone next to them dropped some flowered rain boots on Dad's foot, and Dad was busy saying it didn't hurt at all, even though Rosie could tell by the way Dad was limping that it did.

"Maybe we could get the blue boots this time and pink when your feet grow," Dad said hopefully when the boot droppers had moved on. He looked like his headache was getting worse, and Rosie wanted to help, but there was no way she would ever wear ugly mold-blue boots.

"How about we wait and come later for pink boots?" Rosie said, pleased she had found a good solution. "We can come next week."

"I don't know if I can face coming here again in this lifetime, let alone next week," Dad muttered as a woman pushing a baby stroller nearly plowed them down.

Just then, three boys knocked over the umbrella display, and Dad went to help.

"Did you get your boots, Rosie?" Charlotte asked, coming up with a pair of purple boots in her hand.

"No, they don't have the right ones," Rosie said.

"Where's Dad?" Tom asked as he walked over with boots that were army green.

Rosie was about to tell him when her brother's eyes suddenly got wide and the green boots slid out of his hand.

"It's him," Tom whispered urgently, staring at the aisle behind them.

At first all Rosie could see was a family with four arguing brothers, but then she too saw him, the man from the house. He was wearing the same brown coat and slipping effortlessly through the crowd, unnoticed by everyone except the Baileys.

Charlotte drew in a sharp breath. "If we follow him, we might be able to find out what he's really up to—and get it on video."

"Good thinking," Tom said, taking off after the man. "Just don't let him see you."

Rosie flew after him, Charlotte on her heels, though the crowd made it tough to move fast. Charlotte kept whacking people in the knees with her purple boots and having to apologize while Tom kept stepping on other shoppers.

Rosie was the first to reach the end of the aisle, and she craned her head, trying to see where the man had gone. Unfortunately everyone around her was tall and very in the way.

"He's headed into lawn and garden supplies," Tom said as he came up, slightly breathless.

"Don't let him get away," Charlotte hissed as they took off.

The man did not stop to look at garden tools or grass seed. He just darted past families and lone soldiers picking up supplies.

Before they could follow, the Baileys were cut off by a rogue shopping cart full of cat litter. "We're going to lose him," Tom cried. But Rosie was able to inch past and keep the man in her sights as he nearly sprinted for the automotive section at the very back of the store, near the rear exit. He was probably going to buy engine parts to build an escape vehicle to take the dogs, including Buddy, away forever. Rosie could not let that happen. She sped up and was closing in on the man, when suddenly a security guard reached out and grabbed Rosie's arm.

"I can't let you outside without an adult, little miss," the guard said. Her voice was kind, but Rosie was no "little miss" and the man in brown was getting away. He was already out the automatic doors, and once he made it to the parking lot he would be lost for good, ruining their chance to save the dogs.

So Rosie did the only thing she could think of: She yelled. There were a lot of things she could have said, and later that night Rosie thought of all of them. But in that moment, what escaped her lips was, "IED!"

And as it turned out, when someone, even someone who was only six, shouted about an improvised explosive device in a store full of army folk, the result was pure chaos. People screamed and ran and ducked for cover, and the security guard, in what she believed was a show of valor, threw herself on top of Rosie. The last thing Rosie saw before being buried under the guard's polyester uniform was the man in brown heading out into the sunset.

Later, after Dad had apologized to the store manager for the millionth time, and the Baileys had left the PX in disgrace, Rosie overheard her brother and sister.

"I wish we'd been able to follow him," Tom said, his voice wistful. "Who knows what we might have found?"

"I know," Charlotte said, her voice gloomy. "We'll just have to make sure we get inside the house and get that video tomorrow."

"Yeah," Tom said heavily.

Her siblings thought Rosie had blown it, and Rosie knew it was true. She'd picked the worst time ever to finally get a military term right. As they drove home, Rosie blinked back tears.

She wanted to save the dogs and help her brother, but instead she had messed up everything.

CHAPTER 19

It was a quiet bike ride as Charlotte led the way to the alley off Crimson Drive the next morning, sweat prickling her temples despite the fact that it was barely eight a.m. Their plan was simple: Find a way into the house, sneak down to the basement, and make a video of Tom checking out whatever they found there. Her cell phone was charged and ready for filming, and Tom had brought along Dad's old binoculars. Rosie was ready too, dressed head to toe in spy gear complete with her night vision goggles and Dad's watch with a timer, flashlight, and glow-in-the-dark numbers.

They stowed their bikes under some bushes at the corner of Crimson Drive, then crept slowly through the trees at the side of the alley until they'd reached the house. Charlotte, who was in the lead, raised a hand, and they all came to a halt while Tom used the binoculars to see if there was any movement.

"All clear," he said quietly.

"Okay, then, Charlie Mike," Charlotte said, using the lingo for continuing a mission.

"No more military words," Rosie said sharply.

Well, Charlotte could certainly understand her sister's aversion to them today. "Sorry," she whispered.

They headed to the house, where they began testing windows. Last time only Rosie had attempted to open them so Charlotte was hoping if she or Tom, who were taller and bigger, tried, they might be able to get one of them to budge.

"This one opens partway," Tom whispered. The window was at the side of the house, and Charlotte went to help him tug.

"I think it's stuck," she said after a minute. Sweat trickled down her back, making her skin unpleasantly sticky.

"I can fit in there," Rosie said in her normal voice. "And then I can open the front door and let you in."

Charlotte and Tom quickly shushed her.

"That's not safe," Charlotte said as Rosie glared at them. "Don't worry, we'll find another way in."

She just hoped it was true as she followed Tom around to the back of the house.

Rosie was tired of Tom and Charlotte ignoring her ideas. They didn't believe her about the dognapper, they thought she'd ruined their chances at following the man in brown, and now they didn't think she could open the front door by herself. So Rosie decided it was time to show them—she was going to sneak into the house all by herself. She waited as her siblings rounded the corner, then poked her head into the partially opened window, wiggled her shoulders through, and kicked until she'd managed to wedge her whole self inside.

Rosie stood up fast, in case the evil man was there, but the room was empty. Using her best stealth moves, she tiptoed into the hall where she saw what she was looking for: the door to the basement. She held her breath to be extra quiet as she turned the knob, then pulled the door open slowly. It creaked and Rosie froze. What if someone was in the building? Had anyone heard her? She could make out noise, a kind of soft rustling coming from down below, but whatever was there had not been disturbed by the sound.

Rosie straightened her night vision goggles, then crept through the door. The stairs were narrow, but enough light came in from the small basement windows that the area wasn't dark. Rosie walked silently down two steps, then crouched low and took her first look into the big room below. And then she gasped.

From where she was sitting she could see a cage, and inside it, curled on a blue pillow, was a big German shepherd with a black snout. Buddy. She'd found him at last!

Rosie flew up the stairs to the front door, ready to show her siblings she'd been right about everything the whole time. But in her haste she forgot to look outside first. When she threw the door open, she was shocked and dismayed to see the sinister man coming up the path. He was looking at his phone and hadn't seen her yet, so Rosie stumbled backward, trying to duck back inside. But somehow she hit her wrist, the one with Dad's watch, on the jamb and the timer began, crisp beeps that rang out loudly in the quiet air. The man's head jerked up and he looked straight at Rosie.

Change of plans! Now that she'd been spotted, she just wanted to escape so that she wouldn't be trapped inside with him. Rosie's heart hammered as she raced down the steps toward the bushes along the driveway. But her night vision goggles that had been up on her forehead slid down, blinding her completely. Rosie kept running, hoping she was headed for safety.

And just to be sure the man didn't kidnap her and stuff her in a cage with the dogs, Rosie let out the loudest, shrillest scream of her life.

Tom was pulling on yet another locked window when a deafening shriek pierced the air. He started and nearly shrieked himself.

"What was that?" Charlotte asked. She had been crouched next to him, but now she jumped to her feet.

Tom wasn't sure, but he'd just realized they had an even bigger problem. "Where's Rosie?" he asked.

The scream came a second time, and this time it made Charlotte's face go a scary white. "That's Rosie," she said in a strangled voice.

Tom's insides were clenched up so tight he could barely breathe as he ran toward the sound. And when he rounded the corner of the house he saw something that made his chest feel like it was about to explode. It was Rosie, her night vision goggles covering her face as she stumbled straight toward the man in brown. And he was reaching down to grab her.

It was terrifying, but Tom forgot to be scared. He forgot to screech, he forgot to worry about what could happen, he forgot everything except Rosie.

"Get away from my sister!" Tom bellowed. He raced across the yard, leaped over an old flower bed, and ducked under a low tree branch, ready to do anything and everything it would take to save Rosie.

CHAPTER 20

Charlotte flew after Tom, rounded the corner—and saw the man in brown grab Rosie and lift her up.

"Stop!" Tom was shouting, waving his arms.

"Put her down!" Charlotte screeched, right on his heels and flailing her arms just as wildly.

The man looked at Tom and Charlotte as they stormed up to him. "I just don't want her to hurt herself," he said, setting Rosie gently down and lifting the goggles off her face and onto her head.

Rosie looked around, then hugged Tom tight. Charlotte hugged them both. "He almost got me," Rosie said, looking up at Charlotte and Tom with big eyes.

"You're safe now," Tom assured her, giving the man a fierce glare in case he had any ideas.

Charlotte gave the man her own glare, her arm around her sister.

He lifted up his hands. "She could have tripped over a root or run into a tree with her face covered like that," he said. "I didn't want that to happen."

Charlotte wasn't quite sure what to say or what to make of the man up close. Somehow he wasn't so sinister in the light of day. His brown eyes were kind and they twinkled a bit as he smiled again. Plus what he said was true: They were at the edge of the wooded area, and Rosie actually could have hurt herself. "Thanks, I guess," she said finally.

"So are you the ghosts who were hanging around here the other day, spooking me when I was trying to work?" the man asked. "Because I was beginning to think this place was haunted."

"We're spies, not ghosts," Rosie said. She had let go of her brother and sister and seemed ready to reclaim her dignity.

"Spies, right," the man said knowingly. "So have you figured out what we're doing here?"

"You're a dognapper and you stole Buddy," Rosie said, now fully recovered, her eyes flashing with accusation. "I saw him in the basement, so don't try to deny it."

Charlotte gasped at the news that Buddy was actually there in the basement. Rosie had been right about the dogs all along!

"If Buddy is one of our former MWDs, he might be down in the kennel with the other dogs," the man said. "But I can promise you that no dog in this facility was napped."

"So then what *is* Buddy doing here?" Rosie asked, hands on her hips. "Because we saw cages and meat and you carrying a weapon, and those are very serious things."

Charlotte was beginning to wish her sister had been slightly more traumatized by her scare so that she'd stop spilling everything.

The man's forehead crinkled. "A weapon?"

"It was a big stick, like a bat, with wire on it," Charlotte explained, the memory of it making the man seem slightly more threatening.

The man's face stayed scrunched in thought for another moment, but then he grinned. "Oh, you must mean a heel stick," he said. "It's not wire at the end, it's usually just a leather strap to make it easier to carry."

Charlotte's cheeks warmed at that—how could she

have made such a rookie mistake? Though it *had* been a dark and rainy night.

"We use the heel sticks to teach the dogs the new skills they'll need," the man went on. "I'm Danny Skakov, by the way, head dog trainer and soon-to-be army officer."

Charlotte remembered that sometimes civilians who worked for the army were given officer status if they had skills to offer up. Apparently dog-training skills had landed Mr. Skakov here. That explained his heavy brown jacket too—Charlotte knew that dog trainers had to keep themselves well padded.

The Baileys introduced themselves.

"Can you tell us why they need new skills?" Charlotte asked after they'd finished shaking hands.

"I can indeed," Mr. Skakov said. "Do you kids know what MWDs are?"

"Military working dogs," Rosie said quickly. "They help GIs out in the field."

"That's exactly right," Mr. Skakov said, nodding. "And this is the post's inaugural pilot program to retrain MWDs so that they can be adopted into civilian families."

Rosie jumped up and down. "So you're helping Buddy find a home," she exclaimed.

"Exactly," Mr. Skakov said, his eyes bright. "We're helping all these dogs find homes. They did their time serving their country but suffered injuries that will prevent them from going back out in the field."

"So they're hurt?" Rosie asked, a crease appearing on her forehead.

"We just turned the upstairs into a veterinary clinic to help patch them up," Mr. Skakov said. Now Charlotte understood the syringes and the metal tools: They were medical supplies. And the meat, of course, was just dog food. "And then once the dogs are ready, they come on down to the basement and we begin preparing them for their new lives as pets."

"I bet they'll like their new lives," Charlotte said, thinking of how Cupcake had blossomed in her home after they'd rescued her. "They'll be spoiled rotten."

Mr. Skakov smiled. "That's the plan," he said. "We have five dogs so far and another four arriving later this week, now that we're really up and running."

Tom was frowning slightly. "Why don't their handlers adopt them?" he asked.

"Many times that's exactly what happens," Mr. Skakov said, rubbing his head for a moment. "And we actually have a dog upstairs at the veterinary facility now, waiting for his handler to get back from the hospital in Germany. But in other cases, if the dog comes home early due to injury, the handler starts over with a new dog. Or sometimes a handler is unable to take the dog in after he or she completes their tour of duty." He cleared his throat, and Charlotte realized there was another reason a handler might not adopt a dog: because the handler did not make it home. It was the reality that no military family ever wanted to think about, and Charlotte was glad when Tom changed the subject.

"Why was everything top secret?" he asked.

"We needed the dogs to be able to arrive here in complete quiet," Mr. Skakov said seriously. "After what they've seen in military zones they startle easily and can have issues with crowds. This is a whole new setting for them, and we wanted them to feel as safe as possible during the transition time."

That all made sense. And finally the mystery was solved! There was just one last thing that concerned

Charlotte. "I hope we didn't bother the dogs when we came and looked around."

Mr. Skakov shook his head. "No harm done," he assured them. "In fact, as of this morning they are officially cleared for visitors, and part of their training is exposing them to kids. So I wonder if you three would be willing to help us out and come downstairs now to play with them!"

CHAPTER 21

Tom was not surprised when Rosie started jumping up and down.

"Let's go, let's go!" she shouted. "I want to see Buddy!"

Tom was still reeling from all the new information about the house and the dogs, but he did know one thing: No way could they go into a strange house without permission from Mom and Dad. "We just need to check with our parents first," he said.

"Right, of course," the man said. "Let's give them a call."

Tom pulled out his phone and dialed Dad. Dad listened to Tom's edited version of the story, then asked to speak to Mr. Skakov, who took the phone from Tom and stepped away so he could hear Dad.

"Rosie, you were right, there were dogs here," Charlotte said, turning to their sister.

Rosie puffed up and smiled smugly. "I told you so," she said.

Tom glanced at Charlotte and they both laughed.

"You sure did," he said. He looked at the house, which had once seemed so sinister, bathed in shadow and abandoned. Now the trees surrounding it just provided cool shade on a hot day and the building itself just looked like, well, a building.

"I can't believe we might finally get to meet the famous Buddy," Charlotte said.

"Yeah, I hope Dad says we can go inside," Tom said.

"I'm not leaving till we see Buddy," Rosie said with such gusto that the goggles fell over her face again.

Tom laughed while Charlotte reached over and took them off her sister. "I think these have caused enough trouble for one day," she said. "How about you just carry them?"

Rosie considered, then nodded.

"Your dad gave us the go-ahead," Mr. Skakov said, coming back over and handing Tom his phone. "He'll come meet you here in a few minutes. Are you guys ready to see what we've got going on inside this old building?"

"Roger that!" Rosie shouted.

Tom nodded eagerly, but Charlotte held up a hand.

"We are," she said slowly. "But would it be possible to make a video of it? A video with a few, um, flares? It would kind of save us, if it's okay with you."

Mr. Skakov leaned forward. "I'm intrigued," he said. "Tell me more."

"Yes, the site is secure," Mr. Skakov said, his back facing away from the phone Tom held up. They were standing just inside the house with the lights off, so the image was dark and slightly grainy, just how Tom wanted it. "This is a top secret mission, and no one is going to be able to—" Mr. Skakov turned to face the camera phone, and his eyes widened in a very believable expression of shock. "Hey, how did you get in here?"

Tom made a muffled sound and shifted the phone so that he was in the frame too.

"Don't let him escape," Mr. Skakov called. Tom was pleased to hear how sincere he sounded, as if security had truly been breached.

Sergeant Brogan, an assistant dog trainer who had arrived a few minutes earlier, came charging up the stairs as though she were coming after them. "Stop!" she shouted.

Tom clicked off the video. "Perfect," he said, very satisfied with the take. "Thanks."

"This reminded me of my days in high school drama," Mr. Skakov said. "Though I never got the lead in any of those plays."

"You did a great job with the lead here, sir," Tom said. "You were very convincing."

"I think it's going to be perfect," Charlotte said, grinning at her brother.

"So can we visit Buddy?" Rosie asked impatiently. "He's been waiting a really long time to see me again."

"Is it okay if I take some more video footage?" Tom asked as they headed down the basement stairs.

"Sure," Mr. Skakov said. "We're open to visitors now, and more kids coming by would be great. We'll have a sign-up so that we keep it to a few people at a time. And of course we want families to meet the dogs. Maybe some of them will find homes right here on post."

They'd arrived at the basement to find that in the past week it had been transformed into a small, cozy kennel. Cages with colorful dog beds inside lined two walls. Metal storage bins held training supplies and were secured with the locks the Baileys had seen on the table. There were sticks inside like the ones Charlotte had seen Mr. Skakov carrying, as well as rubber balls, feeding supplies, and leashes, which were the leather straps they'd seen when they'd peeked in the basement window.

But best of all were the five dogs. Two were at the food bowls finishing up breakfast. Another was on a leash with a trainer who was using the heel stick as a guide tool. The fourth was now with Sergeant Brogan, getting a treat for sitting when told to do so. And the fifth, a German shepherd with a long black nose, was bounding up to greet Rosie.

"Buddy!" Rosie shouted, hugging the big dog close. She was rewarded with a slobbery lick on the chin that made her giggle.

"His name in the field was Phantom," Mr. Skakov said, reaching over to pat the wriggling dog. "But Buddy's a good nickname. This guy is about ready to be adopted, Taco and Daredevil too. They arrived in pretty good shape. Pixie and Boots will need some more time here, but they'll be ready soon enough."

Tom saw that Pixie was cowering a bit, and Boots had part of the fur on her back shaved off so that a cut with neat stitches could heal. She too seemed skittish at their arrival. But when the trainer with Taco unsnapped her leash, she headed straight for Tom and Charlotte.

Tom noticed that she limped a bit but her tail was wagging, and she leaned against his legs when he bent down to pet her.

"What a sweetie," Charlotte said, grinning as Taco nuzzled her hand.

"Phantom," Rosie said. "That's the perfect name because me and Victor really thought he might be a phantom."

"He did disappear that day," Tom remembered, looking up from petting Taco.

"Yeah, with that awful lady," Rosie added. She was snuggling Phantom/Buddy but still scowled at the memory.

Mr. Skakov snorted. "I think you might be referring to Private Saunders. Phantom arrived early, so she was charged with his care and was under orders to limit his socialization until we were sure he was ready to mingle with people. Unfortunately he got off his leash and ran away one day. I think she got pretty scared."

"Well, she was very rude." Rosie sniffed. "But I guess she was just trying to take good care of Buddy."

"Yes, I think that was it," Mr. Skakov said with a smile. "And clearly he's pretty happy to interact with people now." Phantom was wriggling with delight as

Rosie rubbed his furry tummy. "So I hope you'll come back to visit him again."

Rosie nodded seriously. "I will," she said. "And my friend Victor will come too. His daddy has a dog named Sunshine, so Victor knows a lot about dogs."

Mr. Skakov, who had been heading over to Boots, turned. "Did you say Sunshine?"

Rosie nodded. "Yes, and Victor was helping me find Buddy. He's going to be very happy when I tell him that Buddy's been here all along."

Mr. Skakov tilted his head. "Yes, you should definitely bring Victor here," he said.

Tom realized he needed to keep filming, and he pulled the phone out of his pocket.

"Want us to be really scary this time?" Sergeant Brogan asked with an evil grin.

Tom laughed. "No, this is the follow-up where we reveal what's really going on." It was important to get this part right, to show everyone that Tom had faced down the danger and truly gotten to the bottom of things. No one would be able to call him Sergeant Wimpy after seeing that.

"Okay," Tom said, holding up his phone. He could just imagine Chase and the others' reactions once they'd seen this. "Let's get started."

CHAPTER 22

"Hurry, hurry!" Rosie shouted. It was later that afternoon, and while Tom worked on editing his video at home, Rosie and Charlotte were biking back to the house off Crimson Drive that Rosie now knew was going to be called the Fort Patrick Canine Rehabilitation Center. And this time, they had Victor with them.

When they arrived at Victor's house, he'd had some news: Pepper was home. The puppy had dug one of her holes so deep that it had provided her with an escape route under the fence. But after a jaunt around post, including some overnights with friendly families, she'd been returned to her home, much to the Jameses' joy. Rosie was happy to hear the Jameses had their dog home, but her news for Victor was even bigger and she couldn't wait to share it.

Rosie hadn't told Victor who was waiting at the Center—she wanted it to be a surprise. But if Victor didn't speed up, she didn't know if she'd be able to hold her secret in much longer.

They finally arrived, and Rosie was ready to race inside. But as soon as they parked their bikes in the driveway, Victor sat down on the lawn. "I think I got a rock in my shoe," he said, slowly undoing the laces.

"Just come," Rosie pleaded. "You can take the rock out later."

Charlotte shot her a look that said Rosie was not respecting Victor's feelings right now, then squatted down next to Victor. "Let's get that pebble out of there," she said, taking Victor's blue sneaker and giving it a good shake. Then she put it back on Victor's foot and tied it while Rosie stood next to them, trying not to explode with excitement.

Finally, finally Victor was ready. Rosie led the way up the steps, and Mr. Skakov met them at the door, with Phantom/Buddy on a leash right next to him.

"It's Buddy!" Victor exclaimed, looking at Rosie. "Right?"

"Right," Rosie said, greeting the big dog with a hug. "Only his real name is Phantom and he lives here now."

Victor looked slightly perplexed as he held out a hand for Buddy to sniff. "That mean lady isn't his owner?"

Mr. Skakov snickered, but Rosie shook her head seriously. "No, Phantom was an MWD and now he'll be adopted."

"This is a really good surprise," Victor said, petting the soft fur on top of Phantom's head.

Rosie exchanged a gleeful look with Mr. Skakov. "It is, but there's more," Rosie said. "An even bigger, better surprise."

She'd found out about it from Mr. Skakov. While Rosie's siblings were making the video, he had taken her upstairs to the veterinary office. And now Rosie couldn't wait for Victor to see what was up there too.

"Can we go now, sir?" Rosie asked Mr. Skakov.

He nodded. "Yes, Major Cho is ready for you."

Rosie wanted to race up, but Victor was a slowpoke again, taking his time to climb up the wide wooden stairs carefully. The top floor of the building was light and airy, with small offices for different veterinary procedures and canine dental work. Rosie led Victor straight back to the big exam area full of chairs, a metal table, and a cabinet of vet medical things, where Major Cho, the kind vet, was waiting. But none of those things were the surprise. The surprise was sitting on a red corduroy dog bed, a bandage around one paw but his tail wagging slightly as he watched them walk in.

For a moment Victor looked at the dog, then he gasped and his eyes filled with tears. "Sunshine," he said, his voice scratchy.

"Yes!" Rosie said, nearly dancing with delight. "He came home to wait for your dad to get back."

Victor walked over to the dog and hugged him tight, burying his face in Sunshine's fur.

Rosie glanced up at Mr. Skakov and saw that his eyes were a bit red. "Don't worry, Victor's happy," she said, patting Mr. Skakov's hand. Sometimes grown-ups got confused, but Rosie understood Victor's tears perfectly because she was getting very good at respecting feelings. "Now Sunshine can keep him company while he waits for his dad to come back."

Mr. Skakov squeezed her shoulder gently. "He sure can," he said.

Later, after Victor came over for a dinner of Dad's famous spaghetti and meatballs and they made s'mores on the backyard grill, Rosie took Victor up to her room to build Legos.

"I sent Dad some pictures of Sunshine," he said, pressing a red brick into the fortress they were just about done making. "Mom said they made him happy and that having Sunshine here will help Dad be less confused when he finally gets back."

"Dogs are very good at helping," Rosie said. Cupcake, who was flopped next to them on the floor, made a snuffling noise as though agreeing. "Will Sunshine come live with you and Aunt Carmen?" She was starting to gather up her army, the green figurines, and set Victor's, the blue, in a separate pile.

"Aunt Carmen wasn't sure at first," Victor said. "Before, the plan was to wait till Dad got back. But Mr. Skakov said it would be good for Sunshine and for me if he came earlier, so Sunshine gets to come next week."

This was excellent news. "Now you'll have a best friend right across the street," Rosie said to Cupcake, who licked her hand. "That will make you very happy."

Victor cleared his throat. "I'm very happy to have my best friend right across the street too," he said.

Well, this was a surprise. Rosie had never had a friend before, let alone a best friend. And she wasn't so sure about having one now. But as Victor beamed at Rosie, his face nice and kind, red eyes and all, Rosie reconsidered. Yes, Victor might not always play what she wanted, he might go too slow, or maybe even try to take charge of things—but when she remembered how happy she was to see Victor with Sunshine, it suddenly didn't seem so annoying. In fact, making Victor happy had made Rosie happy too. Really happy.

So Rosie nodded. "Yeah, me too," she said.

Now that that had been settled, it was time for the war. "Do you want to have your army inside the fortress or attacking?" Rosie asked, knowing it should be his choice since he was the guest, even though she really wanted to defend the fortress.

But Victor shrugged. "It's up to you," he said. "You can be in charge because you're really good at it."

Yes, Victor really was the bestest best friend there was.

★ CHAPTER 23 ★

On Monday morning, as he walked to school with Charlotte, Tom's palms were sweaty and his mouth felt as though he'd eaten wads of dry cotton for breakfast. "Do you think this is going to work?" he asked, checking for the tenth time to make sure he had his cell phone with their video secure in his pocket.

"I hope so," Charlotte said as they waited for a car to pass and the crossing guard to give them the okay to keep walking. She didn't look as anxious to him as she had the past two weeks, so maybe she really was convinced that the video would put Sergeant Wimpy to rest for good.

"Maybe we should have tried to make a video where we scared Chase," Tom said. Suddenly this seemed obvious. Why would anyone care about their silly video? Videos where someone looked dumb were always more exciting—how had he not seen this before?

But Charlotte was shaking her head. "No, ours is perfect just how it is." There was a serious note in her voice that soothed him. And what she said was probably true—but still, was their video enough to undo the damage of what Chase Hammond had done?

They'd reached the big yard in front of the school, so now they would find out. Chase was already there, a small group of boys gathered around him.

"Okay, this is it," Tom said. He could actually feel his legs getting shaky at the thought of walking up to Chase.

"Let's do it," Charlotte said.

"You're coming too?" Tom asked. He couldn't help feeling surprised, considering how she'd been avoiding being seen with him at school. Not that he blamed her, since who would want to be associated with Sergeant Wimpy?

"Yup," Charlotte said firmly. "I've got your back on this."

That helped. A lot. Tom wiped his sweaty palms off on his jeans and, with Charlotte at his side, walked over to where Chase and his friends stood under a big oak tree.

"What do you want?" Chase asked, his eyes narrowing.

"He probably wants to beg for mercy so you don't

scare him with a worm," a boy named Winston said with a snicker.

Chase grinned at this, but his eyes were still narrowed as he looked at Tom.

Tom had his phone out now. "Actually I have a video to show you," he said, glancing at Charlotte, who nodded.

"Me and both my sisters found out what's been happening in that old building off Crimson Drive, the one everyone thinks is haunted," Tom said. "And we taped the whole thing."

"Really?" Winston asked, sounding interested despite himself. Tom saw Charlotte smile.

"Yeah," Tom said, noticing that a few boys including Kenny and his friend Avi had joined the group. "We went inside and everything. There was all this creepy stuff, like cages and syringes."

"Big deal," Chase said. "What's so scary about an empty cage?"

"Um, well," Tom faltered, not sure it was worth continuing, not when Chase was so scornful about every word that came out of Tom's mouth. Had he done anything worth sharing? He nearly backed away.

But then Tom saw Charlotte nodding. He saw that Kenny had moved closer, looking genuinely intrigued.

And that gave him the courage to take a deep breath and push on. "The cool thing is that we found out the army is bringing MWDs there to be rehabilitated and adopted."

But Chase was smirking. "You found puppies in an old building?" he mocked. "I'm so impressed."

Winston snickered again, clearly back in Chase's camp of supporters. Tom looked at the other boys gathered, the way most of them were sneering, ready to jump in and taunt him the second Chase gave the signal. How could Tom explain that empty cages in a gloomy building bathed in shadow *were* scary? And that it had taken real guts to go inside?

The video would not work—Tom saw that now. None of Chase's followers would care about the spooky house, the spy work Tom had done with his sisters, or the truth that they'd uncovered. And suddenly, despite the heat of the day, Tom felt cold.

"Maybe you're scared of dogs, Sergeant Wimpy. I guess they *are* scarier than a little water," Chase went on. "But none of us are." A few of the boys high-fived at that.

So this was it. Tom was destined to be Sergeant Wimpy for the rest of the year if not the rest of his life.

Everyone would think he was a big scaredy-cat, and there was nothing he could do to change it.

But as Tom started to put his phone back into his pocket, he realized something else: Maybe the video had failed, but the process of making it had taught Tom a lot, and the number-one thing on that list? That he was not a wimp. After all, he was standing here confronting Chase—no scaredy-cat could do *that*.

"Wait, you're not going to show us the puppies?" Chase asked, nearly cackling with glee.

Tom *was* brave. He'd gone into the house with his sisters, he'd raced after Rosie when he thought she was in danger, and he'd walked up to Chase today, ready to defend himself. And as he thought about it, Tom decided that maybe being scared was part of being brave, that facing down your fears was the bravest thing a person could do.

"I'll show you some pictures of the dogs if you want," Tom said calmly. "They served our country, and now they're being retrained for adoption, and to me that's pretty cool." As he spoke Tom realized yet another thing he had learned: that maybe being brave wasn't the most important thing anyway. Maybe it was more important to do stuff he genuinely liked and cared about, like hanging out with his sisters, and helping out with dogs who needed new homes, and standing up for himself in a way that was true to who he was. In fact, Tom was pretty certain all those things were a lot more important than proving something to a boy who was wasting his time taunting Tom.

Kenny stepped out of the circle, toward Tom. "I'd like to see your video," he said. He grinned at Tom, then at Charlotte.

Tom had been so worried about Chase that he'd never bothered to talk much to Kenny. Now he remembered how friendly Kenny had been on his first day, and ever since. Because another thing Tom cared about was having friends, real friends, and Kenny seemed like an awfully good candidate. And with Charlotte and maybe even Kenny at his side, Tom wasn't alone anymore.

Tom looked at Chase, really looked at him for the first time. He was still tall and strong, his face was still hard, but now Tom glimpsed something else, something in his eyes that made Tom remember that night at the Officers' Club when he'd heard Chase's dad putting him down. "I'm sorry I got you in trouble with your dad," Tom said, looking squarely at Chase.

Chase's eyes widened and then he ducked his head for a moment. Tom wondered if this might change anything, but when Chase looked at him again it was with scorn. "Whatever, Sergeant Wimpy," Chase said. Then he turned and headed toward school, most of the boys following.

"That's awesome that MWDs are being trained for adoption," Avi said, coming up to Tom.

"Totally," a boy named Erlan agreed. "I want to try to talk my folks into adopting one. Could we go over there with you sometime?"

"That would be terrific," Tom said happily.

The bell rang, and Tom looked at Charlotte, who gave him a thumbs-up. "It worked," she said.

Tom had never even shown Chase the video, most of the boys still thought he was a scaredy-cat, and he was still called Sergeant Wimpy. But despite that, Tom knew that making the video *had* worked, in ways that were way more important than he'd realized until now. So he nodded at Charlotte.

"Roger that," he said.

★ CHAPTER 24 ★

"Did you hear Hope giving all the answers in math today?" Sophia asked, as she and Mari joined Charlotte on the walk to the cafeteria for lunch. "What a teacher's pet."

"She's so full of herself," Mari agreed with a sniff, as she carefully brushed back a lock of her black hair.

They both glanced at Charlotte, waiting for her to agree. But when Charlotte thought of Hope, eagerly answering questions, excited to be getting the word problems that had confused her the week before, she couldn't speak.

"No wonder no one likes her," Sophia said after a slight pause.

They'd reached the buffet area where the greasy scent of overcooked fish sticks made Charlotte's stomach curl up.

Just then, Tash walked by. "Hey, Charlotte," she called over.

Sophia watched Tash walk over to the drink cooler, her eyes narrowing slightly. "How do you know *her*, Charlotte?" she asked softly so Tash wouldn't hear.

"We're neighbors," Charlotte said, tensing up for the attack she could see was coming.

"Oh, well, you might want to stay away," Sophia went on, "just for your own safety. I heard she has to see the school social worker at lunch because she has some kind of mental issues."

Frustration burned in Charlotte's chest, the way it had when Sophia and Mari said untrue things about Tom. But this time Charlotte knew she could not stay silent. This morning she had finally stood by Tom, and she could do this too—she could speak up instead of quietly going along with a lie. She could defend Tash. So Charlotte took a big breath and the words came.

"I think you got the story wrong," she said. "Tash plays the tuba and she spends most lunch periods practicing. And she doesn't have mental issues at all—she's actually really nice."

It was funny because for the past few weeks Charlotte had gotten a delicious fizzy feeling from gossiping with Sophia and Mari, but it was nothing compared to the explosion of sweet euphoria she felt now. Probably because what she was saying now was true, whereas before—well, it had been mean.

Sophia looked at Mari, her lips pressed thin, and a small wave of doubt washed over Charlotte—had she done the right thing speaking up? Yes, telling the truth felt terrific after weeks of nodding along, but Charlotte knew this meant she would no longer be welcome at the prime table by the window, not unless she did some serious backpedaling.

"You guys are not going to believe what Grace's brother just told her!" Jen Sebastian said, rushing up to the three of them, her eyes gleaming. "Get your salads and I'll tell you everything."

Charlotte's hands were trembling slightly, so she looked down at her nails. The night before she'd painted delicate little paw prints on each one, and seeing them now reminded her of the weekend, of finding Buddy, and of the Center and all the good things happening there. Things that were true, unlike the gossip she shared with Sophia and Mari. And remembering that helped her hands stop shaking because she *had* done the right thing speaking up. She was certain of it.

Charlotte cleared her throat. "Actually, I'm not really

in the mood for salad," she said. "I think I'm going to get mac and cheese today." Her mouth watered at the thought because for the first time in a long time, she had an appetite for lunch in the cafeteria.

Charlotte did not look back as she walked over to the hot lunch buffet, took a big plate of mac and cheese, then stood in line to pay.

"Hey," Tash said, coming up behind her. "I heard a rumor that you and your brother and sister saved a bunch of dogs this weekend."

Charlotte laughed. "That's not exactly what happened," she said, handing the cashier her card. "But if I can sit with you today, I'll tell you the real story."

"Sounds good," Tash said. She paid for her lunch, then led the way to a table at the center of the room. It wasn't a prime table, and no one really noticed them as they passed. But to Charlotte, who could finally be part of an honest conversation, it looked pretty good. In fact, it looked like the best table in the room.

Later that afternoon, the Bailey siblings gathered in the backyard. Tom and Charlotte sat on the wooden chairs their parents had brought home the week before, while Rosie lay on the grass with Cupcake.

"You get to play with Sunshine on Saturday," Rosie told their dog as she scratched Cupcake's belly. "And hopefully you'll get to see Phantom soon. That's Buddy's real name."

"So you found Buddy at the Center."

All three Bailey siblings turned and saw Mom, who was dressed in the green uniform she wore to work. "And I hear you made quite a good impression on Mr. Skakov, soon to be Major Skakov," she went on as she leaned against the picnic table and folded her arms across her chest.

"Um, yeah," Charlotte said. It was impossible to tell how much Mom knew. Or if she was mad.

"It was really quite the mission to discover all of that, wasn't it," Mom asked in a way that made it not really a question.

"Yeah, we're really good spies like you," Rosie announced cheerfully as Cupcake jumped to her feet and ran after a squirrel.

"Yes, you've been busy the past few weeks," Mom said. "I kept wondering when you were going to ask for my help."

"So you knew what we were doing this whole time?" Tom asked sheepishly.

Mom laughed. "What kind of intelligence officer would I be if I didn't know what my own children were up to?" she asked.

"But you never told us to stop," Charlotte said, surprised but also not surprised to hear that Mom had been onto them.

"Dad and I considered it, especially when you went near a restricted area," Mom said, raising an eyebrow in a way that suddenly had Charlotte looking very seriously at her feet as she scuffed her toe in the grass. "But we figured we needed to give you some space to make your own discoveries and to make the post your home."

"It worked," Rosie said. "Fort Patrick is my favorite of all the homes we've ever lived in."

Charlotte glanced at Tom, who looked thoughtful but then nodded. "I like it here too," he agreed.

"Even with Chase Hammond giving you a bit of a hard time?" Mom asked, then grinned when Tom's mouth fell open. "We almost stepped in there too, but handling teasing is something worth learning, as long as it doesn't get out of hand."

Tom paused for a moment. "It didn't," he said. "And it won't."

"I'm glad to hear it," Mom said. "But I hope you know—all three of you know—that if you do need help, Dad and I have your backs no matter what."

Charlotte nodded—she *did* know, and she knew Rosie and Tom did too.

"Anybody hungry back here?" Dad asked, coming out of the house carrying a freshly iced chocolate cake. "Because I heard we had one or two things to celebrate."

Charlotte looked at Tom and Rosie, then at her parents. It was true, the Baileys did have a lot to celebrate. In fact, right about now, with the mystery solved, new friends, and a bunch of MWDs to play with, Charlotte thought everything was just about perfect. Sure, it probably wouldn't stay that way for long—problems were part of life, like Dad always said. But Charlotte knew that no matter what came next, the Baileys would face it together.

And *that* was something to celebrate!

ACKNOWLEDGMENTS

The grandfather I never met is buried in Arlington Cemetery. He was a second lieutenant in World War II and later died in a plane crash while serving our country as a diplomat when my father was only two. His legacy in my family was never far from my mind as I wrote this book.

I am indebted to my cousins Betsy Finley, Pat Driscoll, Christy Perry, and Laura Holt, who all shared their stories of growing up on, and in Pat's case serving on, Navy bases. Betsy, I particularly loved your stories about the pool! Sergeant First Class DeWitt of the US Army gave me invaluable advice when I was getting started; and Debbie Reed Fischer, Air Force Brat extraordinaire, generously took the time to give the book a thorough read—I am supremely grateful for her awesome and informative notes. Rebekah Wallin and Celia Lee were essential final readers, and I am beholden to them and their military families for fine-tuning the army-related lingo and facts. All accurate representations are thanks to their help, and any errors are entirely mine.